DOWNHILL

When Sam Sylvester announ... Claribel (a place, not a cow), ... determined to go even though it means selling her pony. David is just as determined, but he has to get a Saturday job and breed some hens to raise the money. Jean, whose father was killed in a skiing accident, is less sure. And Hoomey is certain he doesn't want to go, especially after his mother, who is just as sure he *does* want to go, buys him a pink ski suit.

But the week at Claribel is not quite as any of them expected. Nutty's dreams of gorgeous French ski instructors are quickly dashed when she meets the spotty English youths detailed to give them skiing lessons. David and Jean have an accident and end up trapped on the mountain at night. And Hoomey tastes the high life when Claudine, the local heiress, takes him under her wing, much to his embarrassment!

At once hilarious and exciting, this is, in the words of the *Guardian*, 'a sequel to *Who, Sir? Me, Sir?* and is even better'.

K. M. Peyton was born in Birmingham but spent her early life in the London suburbs and went to Wimbledon High School. After her family moved to Manchester she studied art at Manchester Art School. She taught art for a while but gave it up after starting a family. She has written since she was a child, and has had over thirty novels published, of which the best known and best loved must be the Flambards trilogy, which won the *Guardian*'s Children's Award. She lives in Essex and her passion in life is horse-riding.

K. M. PEYTON

Downhill All The Way

PUFFIN BOOKS
in association with Oxford University Press

PUFFIN BOOKS

Published by the Penguin Group
27 Wrights Lane, London W8 5TZ, England
Viking Penguin Inc., 40 West 23rd Street, New York 10010, USA
Penguin Books Australia Ltd, Ringwood, Victoria, Australia
Penguin Books Canada Ltd, 2801 John Street, Markham, Ontario, Canada L3R 1B4
Penguin Books (NZ) Ltd, 182–190 Wairau Road, Auckland 10, New Zealand

Penguin Books Ltd, Registered Offices: Harmondsworth, Middlesex, England

First published by Oxford University Press 1988
Published in Puffin Books 1990
1 3 5 7 9 10 8 6 4 2

Made and printed in Great Britain by
Richard Clay Ltd, Bungay, Suffolk

1

'Er, um,' said Sam Sylvester.

His class waited patiently. Anything slightly out of the ordinary got him in a muddle, poor man. But they were very fond of him.

'There's a school trip, in March, to—' He fumbled with his notes — 'Um — Claribel.'

Hoomey thought Claribel was a cow, not a place.

'Skiing.'

'Count me out,' thought Hoomey.

Beside him, Nutty's eyes glinted with excitement, flashing through her contact lenses.

'Skiing? Cor, great!'

'Cost for the week—three hundred pounds.'

Nutty's glint died. 'Three hundred quid, sir? For a week! Bloody hell!'

'Um. Rather expensive, I'm afraid. But it includes everything—lessons, ski hire, travelling—'

'I'll say! Concorde for that!'

'Coach,' said Sam.

'My father's,' said Jazz, apologetically.

'What, that old heap? He going to drive it?'

'Of course.'

'Where's Claribel, sir?'

'Er. Um. "Fifteen hundred metres up in the French Alps" it says here.'

'Your dad's coach'll only go downhill.'

'We'll get back okay.'

'Could we get a grant, sir? From the Sports Council?' Nutty was full of good ideas.

'No, Deirdre. This comes under "optional extras".

Optional extras tend to be for the privileged.'

'Rich, you mean.'

'Um. In this case, yes.'

Nutty's father was a greengrocer and was never going to produce three hundred quid out of cabbage sales before March. But Nutty knew she was going skiing. Nutty was a grafter, a square girl of fourteen, built like a tank with a nature to match. She, the girl, was a natural leader of men. Bossy, they said, and ganged up to oppose her. Nutty thrived on opposition.

'Put my name down, sir.'

'You've got to take letters home. You can pass them round, Deirdre.'

Hoomey said he didn't want one. 'You're barmy,' Nutty said, and stuffed one down the back of his neck. It fell out on the bathroom floor when he went to bed and his mother found it in the washing-basket two days later.

'Oh, John dear, what a splendid opportunity! I've talked to your father and he says we can use the money Aunt Margaret left in her will.'

'Oh no, really! I couldn't possibly!'

'No, dear, we've decided we'd like you to go.'

'I don't want to go!'

'Don't be so silly, darling. Of course you must go!'

While this conversation was going on in Hoomey's house, a similar confrontation was taking place in the greengrocer's.

'Don't be so stupid! Of course you can't go!'

'I want to go! I must go!'

'No way, idiot child. Where d'you think I'm going to lay my hands on three hundred quid just after Christmas?'

'I will go! I'll pay for it myself!'

'Fine. Go ahead. Sell that pony of yours if you're serious.'

A stricken silence ensued. Nutty's contact lenses

took off in a sea of tears. She rushed from the room.

'Now look what you've done,' said Nutty's mother to Nutty's father.

'She knows she's got to sell the damned thing. Her feet nearly touch the ground.'

'She loves it.'

'Yes, well, sounds like she loves skiing too. Sell the pony and everything's solved, isn't it?'

A simple, sensible solution . . . Nutty lay on her bed and howled.

2

'Look, John,' said Mrs Rossiter to Hoomey. 'Ski Sunday's on television. Go and watch it while I get the tea. You'll get the idea.'

Hoomey turned on the television, just in time to see a man in orange tights and black goggles hurtle down a snow-chute and take off into a void. Blue sky was all around him. He leaned forward with his arms down close to his sides as if he were standing to attention, and in this unlikely position powered through the sky until a snow-covered ground came up to meet him. Touchdown was accomplished with much yelping from the spectators and crashing of cowbells—the excitement seeming to Hoomey quite in order considering the man had worn no parachute.

'Count me out!' he groaned piteously. But his mother had already filled in the form and sent off the deposit.

3

The catchment area of the Hawkwood Comprehensive was a mix of sprawling seaside town, suburbia in ancient ribbons along arterial roads and godforsaken marshy hinterland where the winds came in from Siberia via the North Sea with a force that withered man and tree alike. Out there, on a farm that tried to grow barley and mostly failed, dabbled in pigs and boasted a rickety shedful of battery hens, David Moore presented the skiing letter to his unsympathetic parents and received the scornful reply he had expected.

'All the same,' he said to his mother grimly. 'I'm going. Dad can't stop me if I earn the money myself!'

'Why d'you think it's so easy—to make three hundred quid? Make enough to scrub along on and you're lucky these days.'

Born losers, David's parents did not command either his respect or his devotion. His father was workshy and a moaner, and his mother accepted their drab lot without complaint. David, according to his report, 'tried hard', which was more than his parents did. He now determined to try hard to make money. He put his name down on Sam Sylvester's list.

'I've got to earn the money myself, but I will—'

Sam looked doubtfully at the stocky freckled boy with the earnest eyes and the habitual air of disapproval of the world around him. David was very much a loner, not unpopular in class in spite of his unfashionable ways.

'I've got some hens, sir. I'll make them pay.'

Sam frowned, disapproving of battery hens and the exploitation of animals—he had visited David's place once and not liked what he had seen.

'I've got some old breeds, silver-laced Wyandottes, and silkies. I'll get the broodies to sit, and sell 'em, sir—they fetch quite a lot of money. They're special, you see. There's still time.'

It was just before the summer holidays—Wyandotte bantams were broody and off lay most of the summer, the main reason they were no longer kept commercially.

'Are they in batteries?'

'Oh no, sir, not mine. Only dad's.'

'Oh, well done. Good luck then. I hope you're successful.'

Sam, known as a bit of a loony leftist amongst the parents, found it difficult to reconcile his ideals with the patently unfair selection of his skiing party—those rich enough to afford it would go; the other poor sods would stay at home.

'Hard to find a spare-time job out where you live,' he smiled encouragingly. 'No paper-rounds!'

'No, sir.'

An idea then occurred to Sam. 'That woman who used to help with the school tetrathlon team—do you remember? She lives out your way. Biddy Bedwelty. She might give you a part-time job. She keeps horses.'

'I could try her, yes.'

Biddy Bedwelty lived a mile down the lane from the Moores. She was a fierce, thirtyish person, said to be female, although it was far from obvious, who trained show-jumpers and dealt in large, stroppy horses. She was a friend of Nutty's. She had agreed to sell Nutty's pony for her, Sam understood, Nutty having decided to make the great sacrifice.

4

'Skiing's great!' Biddy's face cracked into a grin of enthusiasm. 'Of course you must go! Take all the chances that come your way, that's my motto. Me and my sister Betty—we were cracks when we were young.'

David had set off, with some trepidation, to find out if Biddy would give him a holiday job, and found Nutty McTavish in Biddy's yard, having ridden over to leave her pony there. Nutty was in a very subdued mood, which David thought privately was a great improvement.

'What are you doing here?' she asked him.

'He wants a job,' Biddy said. 'The rates I pay, lad, you'll be a grown man before you can afford a skiing holiday. But if you're willing, you can do the mucking out before school. Nails has left me. He's got a job in a racing stable. So I could use you, the way things are.'

'Oh. Thanks.' Looking at her, David wasn't sure whether to be pleased or not.

'Where are you going—for the skiing?'

'Claribel.'

'Claribel? That's a very smart resort! Not the sort most school parties go to. My sister's got a chalet there. Her first husband left it her. I've been there a few times.'

'What's it like?'

'It's sliding down the hill—her chalet, I mean. Not quickly, just a few inches a year.'

'The town I meant.'

'Oh. Full of ladies in pink ski-suits with poodles on

matching leads. Heavenly blokes all sun-tan and aftershave—ski instructors—you know the sort.'

'No.'

Biddy grinned. 'A treat in store! Unfortunately you'll find the instructors who look very beautiful aren't always much good—mostly it's the little ugly ones like monkeys who ski like a dream.'

'*They* teach us—not Sam or Mr Foggerty?'

'Oh, no. You'll have proper instructors. "Bend ze knees!" and all that. You'll go in the beginners' class. They generally have about six or eight in a class—it's a great lark. All falling down the slopes together.'

She laughed her strident laugh.

Nutty said crossly, 'Not falling. I intend to do it properly.'

'Yes, great. All the same, you'll fall. It's much softer than off a horse.'

David, who had thought about it quite a lot, decided to get ahead. 'How do you stop? As it's all whizzing down-hill, if you don't know how to stop, it could be difficult.'

'Good point. They teach you to go slowly and stop before anything else. To stop, you just jump into a sideways position—then of course you stop. But that's pretty difficult, so at first you learn to stop by doing a snow-plough. Just what it sounds like.'

Biddy got down into a straddle position, bottom out, legs apart, knees bent. 'Skis parallel, pointing down-hill, you go faster and faster. Push your heels out and make the backs of the skis splay out, the fronts come together in a vee, and you have your snow-plough. Stops you, doesn't it? Stands to reason.'

Nutty and David were impressed.

'If you knew you could stop when you wanted to, you'd be far more confident, right from the start,' David decided.

'Good thinking,' said Biddy. 'It's the same with horses.'

She grinned amiably. Nutty then got emotional about leaving Midnight with Biddy to be sold and David skived off back home to think about stepping up his poultry production. Life now had an aim, and David knew he was going skiing.

5

'How many takers have you got?'

Mr Foggerty the PE teacher came into the staff-room to find Sam Sylvester filing the replies to his skiing invitations.

'Looks like about twenty. Twelve dead certs and the rest slightly doubtful because of the cost. Some—like David Moore—if he can raise the money himself by January.'

Foggerty picked up the file and riffled through the letters.

'A mixed bag, eh? Jaswant Singh, Sikh, to Darren Wade, punk. Claribel will be agog. Why did you choose Claribel, Sam? It's a real snob place.'

'Frightfully good terms we've been offered. And a chalet specially for kids—we take the whole place over, so there'll be no trouble about disturbing other guests. Madame Dubois—here, look at this—just starting up this business so she'll be on her mettle to give us a good time.'

He handed Foggerty a brochure showing a four-square, smiling Mme Dubois in a pine-framed door-way, holding a basket with some long French loaves lying in it.

'We'll get the real French cuisine, eh, Fred? That lovely hot bread and real Camembert, and those old peasant dishes—cassoulet... wild boar in red wine...'

'The kids'll only eat egg and chips.'

'Oh, go on! We'll educate them before we go. Tell them about the delights in store — the old vin rouge with our dinner — they're not too young to take a glass of wine in the evening, a very civilized habit.'

Foggerty looked doubtful.

'Hmm. Well, you can organize that side of it — the civilization. I'll stick with what I know about. What about the skiing instruction?'

'The chalet supplies the instructors. "Our own young specialists" it says here, "experienced in the needs of younger clients."'

'Hmm.'

'Look, Fred, you might show a little more enthusiasm. I've done all the work getting this trip off the ground. You *are* getting a free holiday out of it!'

'Holiday! Huh! What about insurance?'

'Insurance? It's included, of course. But for heaven's sake, we're not going out there to break our legs! I'm stopping that sort of attitude right from the start. People don't break their legs like they used to, not with the new plastic boots and the improved bindings.'

'Just their necks.' Foggerty laughed like a donkey braying. 'Okay, boyo — sorry if I've offended! It's a great idea. I'm right behind you.'

During the conversation he had been taking in the contents of Sam's file, considering the applications. Some were obvious — Nutty, for her pure determination, Hoomey because of his parents' devotion, young Singh who was a natural athlete — and whose father was going to drive the coach — the well-endowed brother and sister Mark and Sylvie Parker who went to the Mediterranean every summer and had already been skiing several times with their parents, dogged, hard-working David Moore . . . but one application amazed him. He picked out the form.

'Young Jeannie Woods?'

'Her mother says she hopes she can raise the money. It's a single parent family. Her father's dead.'

'I know, mate. He was killed five years ago.'

'Killed? How?'

'By an avalanche. He was skiing at the time.'

6

Jeannie Woods was an intelligent but very quiet and nervous girl with few friends. The brash Nutty McTavish was the object of her envy and admiration: to be so outgoing and so full of ambition and sheer energy filled Jeannie with despair at her own inability to engage attention—well, not exactly attention . . . she was too shy to want that—but she would have liked people to be slightly more aware of her. She had some quiet and mousy friends—or sort-of friends— girls she went around with, but they only talked about boys and make-up and records and Jeannie hadn't yet thought about boys in the way they thought about them, and wasn't into make-up, and the records she liked were apparently all the wrong ones. None of them fancied skiing at all.

'I would like you to go,' her mother said quietly.

Jeannie would have preferred not to. She guessed she would come badly out of the competition—and competition she foresaw it would be. She was not afraid because of what had happened to her father: her father had been way off the beaten track when he was killed, skiing alone, which he knew was foolish. He had taken great risks all his short life and her mother had supported him, unlike the national press who condemned his expeditions as foolhardy. Her father had been a man of few words and much action: a climber, an explorer, an adventurer, and she had loved him very much, what she had seen of him. Her mother had climbed with him in the old days, but was now tied to a nine to five job to keep a roof over their heads, and had lost her old sparkle and sense of fun. A large part of her had died with the loss of her husband, Macey Woods. Jeannie knew she was small compensation and had come between them when he was still alive, preventing her mother going on his crazy expeditions. An ingrained sense of guilt did not help Jeannie's complexes.

'A very difficult child to help,' said her form teacher, Miss Taylor.

But Jeannie did not want help. Only . . . hard to say . . . a feeling that she existed in her own right, an opportunity to make a mark — a small mark.

'Go and enjoy it—not to prove anything,' her mother said, as if she understood. 'Your father had you on skis when you were little. Do you remember?'

She wasn't sure. She could remember her father's face, laughing, his tangled, curly hair flecked with snow, bright sunshine all round him. People had always enjoyed his company, admired him, were shocked by his nerve, and were both sad and smug when his luck ran out. 'He asked for it,' they said. How would all this help her on the trip to Claribel? Not at all, she thought. Her father's name meant nothing to her classmates, only to the clique of men who knew about forcing new routes, or collecting Munros in Scotland or exploring in the Andes.

'We might scrape the money together for you to go, but I don't know about the gear. I'll try and cut down one of your father's duvet jackets to fit—I could shorten the sleeves, at least. He wasn't a big man, after all.'

Jeannie was too loyal to protest, but her enthusiasm

for the trip was not improved by the prospect. Especially as Sylvie Parker was already talking about going to C and A as soon as the new season's styles were in—'The fashion in ski wear changes all the time. I really do want a one-piece this time.'

'Well, you won't look funnier than Jazz, skiing in a turban! Bet there won't be many like him,' sniggered one of her feeble friends.

'Glad I'm not going—his dad driving the coach! What's he going to do all the week? He's not going to ski, is he?'.

Mr Singh was a very large man, large in girth and large in character.

'No, he's not going to ski,' said Jazz. 'He's going to improve his command of the English language. He's taking a lot of books.'

'Oh.' They were impressed. Jazz spoke perfect English with the local dialect, like themselves. Jazz was enviably confident about going skiing.

'S'all right for you,' grumbled Hoomey. 'Your parents just want you to have a good time. Mine want me to come back with a gold medal.'

'Go on! It's you—you're so wet,' Jazz said amiably. 'Always think you can't *do* it. Any fool can ski, stands to reason. Gravity does it. I'm just going to have a bit of fun. Girls, you know.'

Jazz enviably had no inhibitions, in spite of his turban and being brown. He was tall and graceful and quick-witted—everything Hoomey knew he was not. Hoomey was pale and weedy and certainly not into chatting up the girls. The smarty-pants girls like Sylvie Parker scared the living daylights out of him. Nutty was fine; you didn't think of her as a girl, somehow, like Biddy Bedwelty. Just a person. Hoomey had pimples. Jazz's skin was tawny-gold and spotless. Mark Parker—whom Hoomey called Marky-Parky (to himself)—was into girls as well; he was a smoothie, dark and handsome and cocky. He had a friend called Nick Picton (Nicky-Picky Hoomey thought, but did not say) who was coming skiing too—a tall, equally arrogant boy, just as handsome in a golden poetic sort of way, and certainly as conceited. Hoomey felt himself light-years removed from the likes of Marky-Parky and Nicky-Picky. When they all grew up he would be the waiter and they would be the ones snapping their fingers at him; they would throw beer-cans out of their dashing sports cars as they roared past and he would be the man with the dustcart collecting the litter.

He scuffled his feet as he walked across the open space on his way home, thinking all this, unambitious, trailing his schoolbag. Jazz walked at his side.

'They've all been skiing before, you know—the Parkers and the Pictons.'

'So what?'

'They've got those things called salopettes, and goggles and things. The lot.'

'So what?'

Hoomey heaved a sigh. Jazz was magnificently unworried about life.

'Ordinary anorak'll do. Jeans. You look too flash, Hoomey, and all the girls'll stare at you.'

He laughed as Hoomey looked relieved. 'Yeah, that's right. They would, wouldn't they?'

'Mark and Nick, they're going for a good time—girls and that. They reckon they can ski already. Let 'em get on with it, I say.'

Hoomey said, 'Come home with me? We can watch Grange Hill.'

'Okay.'

Hoomey's devoted mother had drinks and cake waiting, all smiles. She waited on her husband and son hand and foot, like centuries back—even Jazz's own Indian mother was not so slavishly devoted to her

13

family as Mrs Rossiter. Jazz often found Mrs Singh watching the children's programmes on the box when he got home from school, although she didn't understand a word. Hoomey's mother never watched the box until her menfolk were fed and tended and happy. Hoomey, the eternal worrier, didn't know how lucky he was.

They settled down on the sofa, scoffing and watching and scattering crisps all over the carpet and cushions, and when the programme had finished Mrs Rossiter came in and said, 'I had a terrific stroke of luck today, John. I was in the Oxfam shop and they had a ski suit just your size—really lovely it is, just like new, ever such good quality. You won't have to use your old anorak after all.'

'Really, mum? That's great!' Hoomey got up, scrunching crisps underfoot. 'Let's have a look.'

'I'll fetch it.'

She departed, to return in a minute with a large plastic carrier.

'Here you are.' Her face was beaming with pride and joy. 'It's just your size—small. It must have been a child's.'

The suit she held up was glossy, bright pink. Right across the back was appliquéd a grinning, bucktoothed rabbit and on the front a teddy-bear.

'Don't worry about the teddy-bear. I can unpick that.'

'Oh, cripes!'

'The rabbit too, if you don't like it. I thought it was rather cute.'

'It's pink!'

'All ski clothes are bright colours, dear. Don't you like it?'

Jazz thought it was horrific. Hoomey was speechless.

'Aren't we lucky? It must have cost a fortune new.

It's quite the thing, a one-piece suit, you know.'

In her delight at her bargain, she failed to notice the marked lack of enthusiasm on Hoomey's part.

'You've nothing to worry about now—we're all prepared!'

She gathered it up and disappeared back to the kitchen.

'Nothing to worry about!' Hoomey wailed.

'You hadn't before, but now—' Even Jazz was doubtful this time. 'The skiing bunny . . . cripes, Hoomey, you'll just have to wear your anorak over the top!'

7

'That lot,' said Nutty contemptuously to Sylvie Parker, with a toss of her knotted black curls towards Sylvie's brother, Jazz and Nick Picton—'All this about having a good time, girls and that . . . what about these ski instructors then? What about writing to this place—Madame Dubois or whatever she's called—and asking her who's going to instruct us? We could get a preview like.'

'Photos! Ask her to send us their photos,' giggled Sylvie.

'Good idea. Then we can choose which class to be in, right from the start.'

'You don't know which is the best instructor by their photos,' Jeannie said uncomprehendingly.

Nutty looked at her sadly. 'That's not the point,' she said gently.

She spread out a great bundle of skiing brochures which she had collected from all the travel agents in town.

'Look. We want an instructor like . . .' She riffled hastily through the well-thumbed literature . . . 'this.'

She triumphantly opened a page to show a bronzed, god-like figure flying off a precipice of snow, black curls flying, white teeth gleaming in an ecstatic smile.

'He's Mario Cellini . . . "one of Claribel's many highly-qualified skiing instructors," it says here. If we put our names down first . . . I mean, s'worth making a bit of effort, isn't it? To get a guy like that. We don't want a *girl* to teach us, do we?'

Hoomey, passing by, saw the photo of the magnificent Mario and noted the skin-tight suit of blue and red stripes—no pink bunnies for Mario Cellini.

'Nice, isn't he?' Nutty demanded.

'Huh.'

In a pink suit with a rabbit on the back, Hoomey reckoned even Mario Cellini wouldn't have the nerve to leap into camera shot. Hoomey planned to break his leg *before* the skiing holiday, even if it meant taking a hammer to it himself.

8

By Christmas Sam Sylvester was able to confirm twenty bookings for the Chalet Clair Ciel, already known to his class as Claridges. He wrote to Madame Dubois, who had already received Nutty's demand for information about her skiing instructors, to confirm the numbers, and the worried lady read the letter over her breakfast table. Her nephew 'Potter' Hawkes, a gawky sixteen-year-old with spots, listened sympathetically. Madame Dubois was none other than Biddy Bedwelty's sister Betty, of the chalet that was sliding down the hill, anxious to make a living since the erratic Jean-Claude Dubois had decamped to Australia with a chalet-girl.

'I wish we'd never gone in for this school booking lark now! Twenty people in the dining-room all at once—it's enough to . . . Oh, Lord! Their insurance cover'll be okay for broken legs skiing, but not for a chalet falling out from underneath them.'

'It's not that bad! At least, the dining-room—' Potter hesitated. The dining-room was built out on a balcony whose supports were the main worry; the town builder had the repairs in hand, but could not do the underpinning proper until the snow melted.

'They'll have to feed in two sittings, all up the top end. At least the bedrooms are all right. Most of the cracks are under the curtains.'

Potter frowned. Since he had taken the castors off his bed it had been all right, but before that he had woken up with the bed against the far outer wall, when it had been against the inner wall when he had dozed off. Objects dropped seemed to skitter downhill into far corners. When one had drunk a couple of glasses of cheap red wine the angles of the doorways and the way anoraks on hooks seemed to hang slightly sideways became very disorientating; the travelling bed could be the last straw. But Potter and his friend Pete, having left school in the summer, had been grateful to get board and lodging with Betty in return for painting and botching the place up. They were enthusiastic skiers and were all set to teach the school-kids when they arrived.

Nutty's letter had got them slightly worried, just as Sylvester's upset Betty.

'They want photos of the ski instructors!' Potter whistled.

Pete returned his worried gaze across the kitchen table. Potter, with his spots, large teeth and mousy, spiky hair, was possibly slightly more presentable than

Pete who had shaved all his hair off for a bet. It was now growing back like a red doormat, one inch long and straight up; he had a nose bent and somewhat squashed in a bobsleigh accident, skin covered in freckles and amiable pale blue eyes with blonde invisible eyelashes. They both wore jeans and long-suffering anoraks of faded colours with tufts of white stuffing protruding out of all the tears and they were perfectly aware that they looked nothing at all like the ski instructors the girls in the letter were hoping for. They could ski happily off white precipices like Mario Cellini, but they didn't look like him while they were doing it.

'If they see our photos, they'll go somewhere else.'

Potter plonked down his ski-pass with his portrait staring back at him from it looking like an advert for a dandruff shampoo. The man the girls didn't want to know.

Pete said cheerfully, 'They can't, once they get here. We'll send 'em some photos out of the brochures. Say they're us. They'll never know. Look.' He grabbed a handful of the literature that was lying about and pored over the pages. 'Here. This'll do. This is me.'

He tore out one of the pages and shoved it over to Potter. It showed a muscled, Batmanlike figure with the obligatory charming smile and pearly white teeth, goggles pushed nonchalantly up against a tousled bush of black curls.

'That's Mario Cellini!'

'So what? How'll they know?'

Potter was impressed.

'The only girl who doesn't love him is—guess who?'

'Claudine!'

'Claudine thinks he's after her money.'

'Of course he's after her money. Everyone is after Claudine's money. Claudine's daddy owns Claribel, after all.'

18

Claribel, once an obscure Alpine village known for nothing but its goat cheese, had been developed as a skiing resort by the hard-eyed, monstrously rich Claude Berthier. His fifteen-year-old daughter Claudine, who asked for nothing but a quiet life, was—unfortunately for herself—stunningly pretty and of an instinctive chic when it came to spending her lavish pocket money on clothes. Everywhere she went covetous eyes followed her: the most eligible girl in France. She was quite friendly with the spotty English boys, because they were far more interested in skiing than girls, and had the wit to sympathize with her situation. Nobody else did.

'Her dad encourages Mario. Because he's an Olympic skier. The more time he spends here the better for Claribel.'

'And the moneybags. Claudine says she's got to be nice to Mario—papa Claude's orders.'

'He's a real shit.'

'Mario or papa Claude?'

'They both are!'

'S'not a bad idea, I suppose,' Pete decided, grabbing the brochure. 'Who'll I be? Gerard? He's not really handsome though. Bit like a monkey.'

'Better than a duck-billed platypus, like you.'

'How about this gink?'

He was studying another glossy smile beaming out of a spray of flying snow. The skier was turning a somersault, a calculated somersault, not the sort Pete occasionally did when trying out a new black run.

'Oh, great!' Potter jeered. 'They won't know about hot-dogging, twit—they'll think that's going arse over tip by mistake.'

'Mmm. I suppose so.' Pete gazed ardently at the picture of the skiing acrobat. It was his life's ambition to be a hot-dogger. 'I'll just cut his face out.'

'Come on, you boys!'

Betty Bedwelty, in shape and demeanour much like her sister Biddy, appeared in the creaking doorway.

'Log-chopping. The logs are all miles too big to go in the stove. We've got to get ahead with all this work.'

They groaned.

'No work. No egg and chips.'

They groaned again.

Betty was no cook and they ate egg and chips, sausages and chips or hamburgers and chips for every meal. 'One of the reasons school kids'll suit us,' she said. 'No hassle with the cooking.'

9

And while Betty was wielding her chip pan in Claribel, Sam Sylvester was regaling his ski class with flights of fancy about French cuisine in Current Affairs.

'These economical peasant dishes . . . simmered over a wood-stove for hours, thick with herbs, pepper, lots of garlic, a dash of wine—pure magic! What a treat in store for you all!'

'Garlic! Herbs!' Hoomey's depression daily grew more profound. If there was no way out of this dreadful trip, he would have to take a suitcaseful of Mars bars and crisps to see him through, otherwise he would starve to death.

The girls at the back were tittering over some photographs they were passing round between them. Ski instructors, tossing their white teeth against the cloudless sky.

'How come, if there's all that snow to ski on, it never seems to be anything but sunshine in the photos?'

'It snows in the night, stands to sense.'

Nutty had an answer for everything. She had sold

her pony for a lot of money and, having got over the grief, was now cockier than ever. She poured scorn on Hoomey for being so unenthusiastic about skiing.

'How'll you ever get any fun, never wanting to do anything? You'll grow up so *boring*!'

'You can be happy without doing things. My grandad's the happiest person I know, and he doesn't do anything at all. Only potter in the garden.'

'I bet he's *boring*.'

Hoomey considered. Boring he might be, but his company was a lot more restful than Nutty's.

'No. He's all right. S'pose *everyone* wanted to go skiing? The mountains'd be worn away. One less, if I don't go—it all helps.'

'That's a very interesting ecological problem, Rossiter,' Sam said earnestly, homing in on their conversation. 'In fact, the boom in skiing is seriously eroding the mountain environment. The growth of ski runs over the high pastures—the compacting of the snow so that it takes much longer to melt in the spring—this is affecting the alpine pasture.'

'Well, you're not helping, sir, taking us lot.'

'One has to measure the value of the experience of skiing as against the effect on the environment . . .'

Hoomey realized he'd set Sam off. His eyes glazed over. They all thought Sam was not quite all there in the top storey, although he was very sweet. He had a girl friend called Big Brenda, who taught Biology, and she kept him in order fairly efficiently. She was coming on the ski trip too. This was a relief, as it was a worry to think of Sam being unleashed on a foreign country without a keeper (especially on skis). They none of them wanted the job.

After he had exhausted the ecological problems of the Alps Sam waylaid David Moore to find out how his finances were progressing. Madame Dubois would shortly be needing the full amount of the cost and

21

David had not yet produced his money.

'It's all right, sir. I've got six trios to sell—that's a cock and two hens—and there's an advert in 'Poultry World' next weekend—I should sell 'em okay.'

'Good lad!'

Sam approved of initiative and self-help.

David went home to feed his ski-trip. It was difficult now the days were so short to get home before they had gone to roost. But only a couple of them were inside on the perch and they jumped down and came running as soon as they heard his voice and the rattle of the bucket. He spread the food about and watched with satisfaction as they pecked away. They were beautiful little birds—white, with each feather out-lined in black. The cockerels were old enough now to start fighting, but so far there had been no damage: he had timed the project to perfection—the birds ready to sell a month before the ski-trip, and all set to start laying at the first hint of spring.

They ran loose around the place during the day and were shut up in the old shed at night to keep them safe from foxes. There were always foxes . . . they bred each spring and had no natural enemies, save the hunt. His father was too lazy to shoot them—besides, one had to be a good shot to kill a fox cleanly. David hated to see half-shot ones dragging themselves around the outbuildings, looking for easy food. The hunt did the best job, whatever the likes of Sam Sylvester said about them. They either killed them or left them in one piece, that was all there was to it.

Once, a hunted fox had come into their yard and killed one of his bantams in passing, the hounds no more than a hundred yards away. It had then jumped up into the straw stack and laid low; the hounds had come into the yard and started casting around and the battery hens had set up such a squawking that his father had come out and told the huntsman to clear off and take his blasted hounds with him. The huntsman did so, and ten minutes later David saw the fox jump down and trot away the way he had come, licking his chops as he went.

David had told this story to Sam Sylvester and Sam had flatly refused to believe that the fox had taken the bantam while being hunted. 'It must have jumped up right under his nose.' David said the fox had stopped and gone back in its tracks to catch it. Sam had put on a distant face and changed the subject. He professed to be a great country-lover and belonged to all sorts of societies for telling farmers what to do with their countryside, but he'd never got really wet or muddy in his life, David reckoned.

He went in and got his own tea, and shut the bantams' door when it was dark and they were all roosting. Then he watched the telly, did his homework and went to bed. It was January and freezing cold. There was a full moon blurred behind the rim of ice on the windows and David lay thinking of the mountains above Claribel . . . he pictured them under this same full moon, the snow-slopes glittering as the surface froze beneath the same bright stars he could see amongst the branches of the dead elm. Although the sea was only a mile away from his home, David had never thought much until now about what lay on the other side. He did not like his home much, although he liked living on the land and farming. The thought of seeing those majestic white mountains against the clear, thin blue of the Alpine sky as depicted in Nutty's ski brochures thrilled him intensely now the date of departure was so close. He liked to lie and think about it at night, when he was alone and quiet. It was rare to have something to look forward to like that.

Perhaps he slept too well. He heard nothing.

He got up and went out into the frosty morning to feed his bantams. The shed was silent, although it was already light. As he fiddled with the frozen catch on the door, he knew something was wrong. Knew what, with a great sick lurch of anger in his throat, half a sob. He flung open the door.

Daylight grinned through the back of the shed where a plank had been broken through. There were feathers everywhere, two dead hens and one dead cockerel with its head bitten off.

David dropped the bucket with a wail of grief and ran round the back of the shed. There was a trail of feathers to the far ditch, and splatters of blood, a few drifting white feathers in the far plough. David ran across the plough, sobbing with rage.

'You bastard! You dirty, murdering bastard! I hate you! I hate you!'

His voice choked on anguish. He ran wildly across the plough until he was exhausted and then went back to search the ditch. He found one hen, the smallest bird called Minnie Mouse, bloodstained and bedraggled but with a breath of life still in her body. One beady eye opened momentarily as he picked her up tenderly. He nursed her inside his jacket and went indoors, crying. He opened the kitchen stove and knelt in front of it, cradling the little hen in his hands, feeling her heart struggling beneath the bloody feathers. He held her up to the warmth.

'Why, whatever have you got there?'

His mother came down and took in the story while David wept. She was full of sympathy and resignation.

'You know what they are, the devils. It's the cold. All gone, are they? That's your little trip, isn't it?'

'I'm going. I don't care what, I'm going!' David gritted out. His tears splashed down on the hen.

'I'll get a box and a bit of warm flannel in it. Put her in the airing cupboard. Come on.'

They always died of shock, in her experience. Although you could never tell with a hen. This one staying alive was neither here nor there, save it gave David something to think about. All his hard work was ruined and wasted.

'I dunno why God made foxes.' She put the kettle on. 'Like flies.'

David laid the little hen in the warm box. He saw the fox in his mind's eye, grinning. The fox-cubs had been lovely in the spring, playing in the scrub beyond the barley-field. He had lain there in the evening watching them once. They had never seen him. Carter the huntsman loved foxes with passion, but his foxhounds as much, and spent his life pitting one against the other. The people who galloped behind were just a joke, out for a ride, but Sam said you could see the blood-lust in their eyes.

Last night the blood-lust was in the fox's eyes.

'I'm not going to school,' he said. 'It's no good.'

The way he felt he would never go again.

'Have a cup of tea,' said his mother. 'You'll feel better.' She poured it out, still in her shabby dressing-gown and carpet slippers. 'But don't think we're going to raise the money for that trip, now your hens have gone. You'll just have to go without. That's all there is to it.'

The little hen blinked at David and gave a last tiny squawk, opening her beak, and died.

10

When David went back to school he told Sam he wouldn't be going on the ski trip.

'A fox got all my birds.'

Sam was very upset. He went to the Headmaster and asked if there was some sort of bursary which could be used to finance David, but the Head gave him a pitying look and said no, not while the roof was falling in and there were ten stolen typewriters to be replaced. David said he didn't care. He hadn't really wanted to go very much. He was surly and rude; Sam couldn't make him out.

'You *do* want to go, don't you?' Nutty asked him belligerently.

'What's the good? All right for some.'

'I got two thousand pounds for my pony,' Nutty said casually. 'I got it in the bank. I'll lend you the money, till you breed some more hens.'

'Don't be daft!'

'It's not daft.'

'Your parents wouldn't let you.'

'It's *my* money, isn't it? *I* made that pony worth two thousand pounds—*I* taught it to jump, didn't I? It only cost three hundred and fifty, so I did . . .' slight pause for arithmetic, 'one thousand, six hundred and fifty pounds' worth of work on that pony. *I* did it, not my mum and dad. It's *my* money. *I* am perfectly happy to lend you three hundred quid until your hens come up again.'

She glared at him, defying him to refuse. No wonder her poor pony had jumped when she told it to! David said he'd think about it.

He did think about it. He couldn't think about anything else. He told Biddy Bedwelty of the offer while he was mucking out her horse, Another Cracker. Another Cracker did enough droppings every day to fill two large wheelbarrows. David was on the first, in the morning, forking diligently, when Biddy brought him a cup of tea. During the pause, he told her.

'Good offer,' Biddy said. 'Take it.'

He was silent.

'Think big. Nutty thinks big. Once she owed me over a thousand pounds, for training, but she didn't let

26

it get her down. She'll think you stupid if you don't take her up on her offer.'

Long pause.

'It would be stupid. Wouldn't it? Not to go?'

David hated the idea of borrowing off Nutty, but going skiing had become a goal for him, a sort of door to a different world, to find out what went on beyond the muck of Marsh Farm. His parents had never taken him away in his life. He was really ignorant about how one went about travelling; what did you do when you got to the other end? This school trip was a magic way of going, without anything to worry about. And the pictures of the white mountains haunted him; he could think of nothing else.

Biddy said, 'You want to take all the chances that come along, lad. You might not get another like this in a hurry.'

David went back to forking the dollops in the barrow, but afterwards, when he went to school, he told Nutty he'd take her up on her offer. She beamed at him, all approval, and told him she'd give the cheque to Sam the next day. His parents were furious when he told them. His mother rang up Nutty's parents, but got no joy. They said Nutty could do what she liked with her money; it was nothing to do with them. This baffled David's mother, and she didn't pursue the matter, although she grumbled on and off for days.

But David, having made the decision, felt as if a great weight had been lifted from him, and counted off the days to their departure with an impatience he had never experienced before.

11

The old bus ground doggedly up the mountain road in low gear. Hoomey, bleary-eyed, had made the mistake of sitting on the right-hand side of the aisle and, as everyone in France drove on the wrong side of the road and the road they were following was winding up the left-hand flank of a steep-sided valley, every time he looked out of the window he saw nothing but a sheer drop below into a gorge through which a ferocious torrent ran, its white teeth gnashing anxiously for human flesh. Or so it seemed to the already exhausted Hoomey. As other buses coming down from the mountain filled the road ahead Mr Singh edged out to the last millimetre until the snow-laden tops of pine-trees swayed below the hub-caps, and Hoomey had to turn his face inboard, so scared that the prospect of racing down a firm snow-slope on skis seemed like bliss in store. Even Marky-Parky and Co. were oohing and aahing and jumping about to look, until Big Brenda told them to sit still.

The landscape seemed quite impossible: wanton and barbaric. Hoomey was not prepared for such foreignness (the Rossiters always went to Bourne-mouth). The road wound upward with fearsome ambition, through tunnels of rock and with breath-taking precision into the chasms and gullies that scored the hillsides, and out the other side, juddering round the hairpin bends. Snow clung where it could on the steep sides of the valley, but ahead and in gaps where streams broke through from the side, high slopes of gleaming white could be glimpsed beyond, unbroken by rocks and high above the tree-line.

Hoomey wouldn't look. He felt sick and the thought of all the Mars bars in his hand luggage made him feel sicker still. They had crossed the channel in flat calm conditions and travelled in the coach all night, sleeping fitfully, and now, in the early afternoon, were on the last leg for Claribel. Sam, having slept soundly, was now full of rapture for the beauty that surrounded them, but Big Brenda, who had slept not at all, was getting more tetchy by the minute. She wasn't the shape for skiing, Hoomey thought. One of the PE teachers, Miss Knox, had come along as well, Foggerty having had second thoughts. She was fierce and hearty and daunting. Not one of them was motherly and sympathetic, as far as Hoomey could see, and the chance of skiving out of the impending athleticism looked remote. Less than twenty-four hours out from home, Hoomey was already desperately homesick for his homely suburb and the soothing flicker of the telly screen, the smell of chips frying and the howls of their neighbour's neurotic dog.

'We're nearly there!' someone said.

There was a signpost, a turn-off, and a road ahead that seemed to break out into a high wide valley clear of gorges and torrents and snapped-off trees. The sun poured down; there was a friendly-looking village with wide streets and coffee-shops and shop windows full of cream-cakes, and above the snow-laden roofs the cabines could be seen swinging up the mountain-slopes carrying hordes of brightly-garbed people. To the bemused Hoomey, it actually looked quite accept-able. The fact that the bus was no longer hanging over the edge of a precipice helped a lot.

Mr Singh stopped to ask the way and they were directed higher up the village over a bridge and up a street that climbed steeply up to a cable-car station. On either side old-style chalets huddled in picturesque

29

Christmas-card style beneath their blankets of snow, and Mr Singh's ancient bus juddered thankfully to its final halt where the road gave out. The Chalet Clair Ciel was the last on the right, its back to the river, a curl of blue smoke drifting from its chimney. It looked decrepit but welcoming. One end of its upper balcony had come adrift and was hanging down. Some spotty boys were looking out through a ground floor window.

'Where's Mario Cellini then?' Nutty had gathered her belongings and was off the bus first. 'Is there time to start skiing now?'

'You have to go to the ski hire shop first,' Sam said. 'Get your boots and skis. And we've got to organize the lift passes. The first lesson will be in the morning.'

'We must sort out the rooms first,' said Miss Knox bossily.

'We've decided that already—who's sleeping with who,' said Nutty.

'We'll see, Deirdre.'

Miss Knox had eyes like glass chips; one did not argue. She was a hockey-player for England, stringy and wiry and fast on the wing. Hoomey shivered whenever her shadow fell near him.

'I'm sharing with you,' he said to Jazz. He needed Jazz's support quite desperately.

They fought their way out of the coach, stumbling out into the sharp air. The snow, piled in heaps on either side of the road by the snow-plough, had alleys through to the front doors. They slithered toward the portals of Chalet Clair Ciel, where a four-square, unFrench-looking woman awaited them, who looked amazingly like Biddy Bedwelty.

Hoomey got trodden down in the rush. The chalet rocked and creaked to the gallop of feet and the hanging balcony lurched still lower, depositing a load of snow on to an unwary passer-by. Hoomey saw Madame Dubois' features betraying dread and alarm, although she said not a word. She backed into the kitchen where Hoomey saw the two spotty boys hunched nervously together, listening to the mayhem upstairs.

'School kids are awful,' one spotty boy said to the other, and they shook their heads glumly.

Who were they? Hoomey wondered. While he dithered, not sure where to go, Big Brenda appeared in the front door, very red in the face and upset.

'Madame Dubois, please help me! Mr Sylvester has had an accident—he's slipped in the snow, and seems to have hurt his ankle—he can't get up!'

'Already! But—'

They all rushed outside and Hoomey followed, agog with curiosity, to find old Sam sitting on the pavement, very white about the gills, and looking sick with embarrassment.

'I just slipped—but . . . oh dear, it's very painful!'

The two spotty boys were down on their knees together, impressive in their expertise. How many broken ankles had they coped with in their short lives, Hoomey wondered with dismay?—dozens by the look of it. They had Sam's shoe off and his trouser leg rolled up, running practised fingers down the bones.

'It's a fracture,' said one.

'The tibia,' said the other.

'Only greenstick. But it'll have to go in plaster.'

'Oh, no!' Sam wailed.

'Oh, Sam darling!' Big Brenda hugged him as he sat incongruously in the snow. 'Poor darling!'

Hoomey thought, if he'd put his foot in just the right place, like Sam, he too could have broken his ankle and the whole holiday would have taken on a much rosier prospect. He watched while they got Sam to his foot and carried him expertly to a van parked in the street.

'We'll get it patched up right away. They take no

time at the clinic. We'll be back in an hour.'

They drove off, leaving Brenda wringing her hands on the pavement. Hoomey suspected he saw a glint of sardonic amusement in the hard eyes of Madame Dubois, although she was making all the right sympathetic remarks. Miss Knox came downstairs and was duly staggered by the news.

'My God, that's ridiculous!' she cried, voicing the obvious. 'Getting out of the bus—! I don't believe it!'

When the news got around, everyone's reaction was similar. The less sympathetic nearly died laughing, rolling on their dishevelled, hard-won bunks. All the pushy people had got the arrangements they wanted; magic Jazz had got the best room of all for himself and Hoomey, one with only two beds in it.

'It's smashing. It runs downhill.'

Jazz demonstrated by dropping his roll of well-chewed chewing-gum on the floor, where it rolled tackily from one end to the other across the bare boards. Outside the window was the wrenched-off balcony. Pinned across the glass was a notice which said, 'Danger. Do not Climb Out.' Someone had pencilled below, 'Polar bears at large.'

Hoomey, feeling better now that he had a base, stacked his Mars bars on the dressing-table. There were twenty-one. At three a day, he could possibly survive on Mars bars alone. The room was gorgeously hot, spewing out central heating with a comforting roar. Next door Marky-Parky and Co. were throwing out David Moore, although they had an extra bed.

'No bloody smell of dung in here, lad. Take it to a country-lover.'

Nick Picton was laying out his after-shave and deodorant. They had their own skis propped against the wall, and had their own boots laid out with their chic ski-suits. David tried a few more rooms and came

32

to Jean Woods in a room of her own under the sloping roof, very small and peasanty. But two beds were squashed in it.

'You can sleep in one,' Jean said. 'We can use the bathroom to dress in.'

It was right opposite, very handy.

David slung his case on the bed. Miss Knox came up and said he was a lunatic. Boys and girls could not—emphatically not—sleep together.

'It's not a double bed,' David pointed out.

'Don't argue. Go.'

Jean and David thought her ridiculous, but David duly departed. Madame Dubois was prevailed upon to produce a folding bed which was put up in the downhill room bagged by Jazz. Neither Jazz nor Hoomey objected. Jean had the peasanty room to herself and was ecstatic at her luck, having dreaded the company of Sylvie and Co. or the admirable but wearing Nutty McTavish. She stood at the window and looked out, entranced by the rose-flushed mountain tops, lit by the sinking sun, that soared above the village opposite her viewpoint. Their serene beauty dazzled her. For all the bustle below and the antlike figures zooming down the lower slopes, the tops were quite inviolate, a world apart. She knew that this was the quality that had compelled her father to take himself into this remote landscape, its attraction like a magnet to him so that he had surrendered everything to its pull. Even his life. For the first time, she sensed that she knew what had lain under his surface of fun and flippancy, why he had disappeared for such long periods, although he had been devoted to both of them, herself and her mother. She was at liberty now to stand and think about all this, which seemed a great comfort, suddenly. She felt very close to her father and, in a strange way, comforted that he would always be as she remembered him: young and agile and funny. She felt very at home, not homesick at all; in fact, just the opposite. As if she had come home.

12

When the spotty boys came back with the pale Sam, his ankle now in plaster, a pair of crutches to hand, his class was congregating in the dining-room, fighting over the best places at table.

The familiar smell of chips and hamburgers cooking cheered the guests enormously, having been prepared for the gruesomeness of French Provençal cooking, as raved over by Sam. Sam sat not quite believing what was happening to him: the hamburgers were an added shock. The holiday had not yet started, but seemed to him to have run out of control already.

The tables were lavishly supplied with tomato ketchup and various brown sauces in gummy bottles, and when comparative silence had descended, eating having commenced, Madame Dubois made a short speech of welcome. The welcome was really a mere preamble to the kernel of her message.

'As perhaps you will appreciate, this chalet is very old and I am appealing to you to treat it with respect. In particular, it is absolutely forbidden for anyone to cross to the far side of this dining-room. The stilts that support the floor have been eroded by the high floods in the spring, and the builders have not yet started work on repairing them.'

'She doesn't sound French to me,' Nutty remarked. 'She sounds just like us.'

Sam was looking alarmed, another problem having been added to his list.

'And I was going to take you all down to the ski-hire

shops after tea, to get you fitted out. I don't know—'

'We'll take 'em, sir,' said the ginger spotty boy. 'We know 'em down there. It'll be best if we do it.'

'Why?' Nutty asked him. 'You live here?'

'Yeah, we live here.'

'What do you do? Are you still at school?'

'No. We teach skiing.'

'You're not teaching us though.'

'Yes, we are. What else d'you think we're here for?'

Nutty put down her knife and fork in horror and, too late, Pete remembered the photos they had sent out of the magazines.

'You!'

Peter was shaking the sauce bottle with great concentration. Nutty rounded on him furiously.

'You sent photographs! That's false pretences! It's against the law, to mislead the consumer—we can sue you—'

'Try it,' Pete said.

Nutty glowered at him. 'You're only about two years older than us.'

'A lifetime of experience,' said Potter.

'We thought—'

'We sent you photos of—' Pete hesitated. 'Who was it? Cellini?'

'Mario Cellini.'

'Well, he's here. We'll introduce you. We can't do more than that.'

'When. Tonight?'

'If you like. If we meet him.'

'You'd better.'

'After we've got our ski things?' Sylvie asked him.

'Yes.'

Sylvie had already got her own skis and boots, but wasn't going to miss this introduction.

'I'll come too then.'

'I'll come as well,' Hoomey said.

35

'We'll all come,' said Jazz.

Hoomey was much cheered by the hamburgers and chips, and set off cheerfully for the gear shop when they had finished, with Nutty and her band, Jazz and David and the spotty boy Pete. The village was brightly lit and busy, the mountains shrouded by darkness, the air sharp. They scrunched down the snowy pavement, and could hear the turbulent rushing of the river that ran behind their chalet, as insistent as traffic noises at home. All the shops were open and thronged with people, and fragrant smells of cooking wafted on the evening air from restaurants, hotels and flats. Everyone was dressed in exotic and outlandish gear to their fresh eyes: in ski-suits and fur coats, ridiculous woollen hats, white jeans, black goggles . . . Hoomey began to think that even his awful rabbit suit would pass unnoticed. There seemed to be a good number of the brochure sort of young men about, tanned faces and white teeth gleaming; the girls kept nudging each other . . . 'Look at that one!' 'Hey, coming towards us, next to the kerb . . .' and 'That one in the green anorak.' Hoomey thought they were hopeless. Their giggles embarrassed him. As if anyone wanted to get tangled up, at their age . . . He walked apart, and did not notice when Pete right-wheeled into the ski-hire shop. He had to backtrack, looking for them, feeling rather foolish.

Nutty was sitting down trying on ski-boots already, and chatting up the young man who was fitting them, another bronzed and elegant youth—although, at close quarters, with rather buck teeth.

'This is the Clair Ciel lot,' Pete said, lounging in a chair by the counter. 'There's nineteen of 'em. They've been paid for already.'

'Yep.' The young man nodded. 'Sit down here,' he said to Hoomey.

He measured Hoomey's feet with a metal footprint

thing, and fetched him a pair of bright red boots made of shiny plastic, about size fifty, by the look of them. They opened on a sort of hinge. Hoomey stuck one foot in, and the boy snapped up the front with a ratchet and chain affair. He brought the other one.

'Stand up. Try them.'

It was like walking in lumps of dried cement. Hoomey staggered down the length of the shop and back. Nutty had now appropriated the youth and was chatting him up.

'What's your name?'

'Carl.'

'Are you French?'

'No. My mother's English. My father's German. Those comfortable?'

'Yes. They're all right. I'd rather have red though, like Hoomey's.'

'Sorry. Colour doesn't count. No red in your size. Go and see Jean-Pierre for the skis.' He turned back to Hoomey.

'Okay?'

Hoomey had no idea whether they were okay or not.

'They're awful.'

Carl grinned. 'You'll get used to them. When you walk, open them up. It's easier. Skis next.'

Jean-Pierre on the ski counter was getting the Nutty treatment, and responding by telling her the story of his life in very strange English.

In answer to Nutty's 'Will you take me to a disco? Tomorrow?' he was saying, 'No, I am in love with another.'

'Who's another?'

'Claudine Berthier. Elle est magnifique!'

His eyes were sparkling. He went through a great mime of passionate embrace to the empty air, then fetched a screwdriver and started to screw Nutty's booted feet down to her skis.

37

Nutty was laughing. 'Does Claudine Berthier love you?'

'No, hélas! Claudine Berthier a le coeur de pierre.'

'What's that mean?'

Pete said, 'Claudine Berthier has a heart of stone.'

'I haven't,' said Nutty. 'You could take me to a disco and forget.'

'I am enslaved for life,' said Jean-Pierre.

He and Nutty were obviously enjoying themselves. Hoomey, waiting patiently, wiggling his toes inside the plastic boxes, said to Pete, 'You know Claudine Berthier?'

'A bit. She's nice to English guys. She doesn't care for all these passionate froggies. They chase her all over town. Her dad owns the place and all these passionate froggies want to marry her for her ski resort.'

'Lor'.'

'She has to fight 'em off.'

Hoomey was impressed.

Nutty had exacted a date out of Jean-Pierre for tea in the Coq d'Or tomorrow. He would tell her all about the depth of his passion for Claudine, and she would buy him a mille-feuille and a hot chocolate.

'Next please.'

He dropped a pair of skis down in front of Hoomey and Hoomey had to put the toes of his boots into the metal toe-clip on the skis.

'Press your heel down.'

He did so and with a click a metal grip homed-to on his boot and fixed it fast to the ski. Jean-Pierre fiddled with the screwdriver.

'That's it. To release it you press this with your ski-stick.'

He gave Hoomey a pair of matching ski-sticks and told him to press the release behind his heels. Hoomey did so, and walked off his skis. It was all rather clever.

And quite easy in the carpeted shop. They staggered out with their unwieldy loads, and Pete showed them how to carry their skis on their shoulders, points down. The boots were awful, with nothing to get a grip on, and it was uphill all the way back once they had crossed the river . . . Hoomey thought he was near death by the time they reached the chalet.

But Nutty said, 'Now for the night-life—and Mario Cellini!'

'Oh Gawd!' said Pete.

'You promised!'

'Okay. Okay.'

Hoomey didn't stand a chance.

13

Claudine Berthier sat in a corner of Piggy's bar with her friend Pascale, drinking citron pressé and hiding behind a copy of *Elle*. Pascale was slender and dark and looked like a gipsy boy; she was cheeky and abrasive and a great protector of the pestered Claudine. Claudine's suitors had to get past Pascale first and Pascale wasn't easy; she was a French version of Nutty and, at sixteen, was on the verge of skiing for the French women's team. Her detractors swore she was really a boy. She had short smooth hair, an olive skin, and scornful brown eyes.

Jazz thought she was beautiful.

'No, you dope. It's the other one, the blonde behind the magazine,' Pete said. 'That's only Pascale.'

'I like that one.'

Mark and Nick were already there, sampling French beer. They brought their glasses over to join them, wanting Pete's expertise.

'This stuff is awful, isn't it?'

'The beer? I only drink lemonade.' Pete was in strict training.

'Shove up, little one.' Mark squeezed in beside Hoomey on the bench against the wall where he had the best view of Claudine—or rather, Claudine's magazine.

'What about Mario Cellini?' Nutty challenged Pete. 'That's what we're here for. You said—'

'He's not here, yet.'

'Is he coming? You said—'

'You'll smell him when he comes in,' Potter said, coming over with a glass of milk. ''S'like a woman's hairdressers—real pong.'

'Gerard's here, if you want a real skier,' Pete said to Nutty. 'That little one at the bar, with dark curly hair. Pale blue sweater.'

Nutty looked. 'Face like a monkey?'

'Mmm. Well. A nice monkey. He won the Men's Downhill here at the Festival. He's ace.'

They sat taking it all in. The music was the same as at home, and the lights and the noise, but it had a definitely foreign feel about it. Hoomey could not stop yawning, the heat inside after the cruel nip in the streets swamping him into semi-consciousness. The others seemed to think it very exciting and macho and sat watching the glamorous men coming in and out. Hoomey had a pang for his teddy-bear, which lived on his bed, which he hadn't dared bring.

Mark said to Pete, casually, 'What happens if you go over and ask the famous Claudine if she'd like a drink?'

Pete said, 'She'll smile, but Pascale will lay into you—all very loud, in French. It's very embarrassing. Try it.'

Mark looked discouraged.

'They're looking at us though,' he said.

'Yes, well, you're new. It's only a small place. They don't like to miss what's going on.'

Claudine was saying, 'They can only be English. You can tell. A school, I bet.'

'That dark one's all right,' Pascale decided.

'That little one—he wants his mummy.'

'We could join them—Pete's with them, after all. Then if Mario comes in he won't pester you. He doesn't like kids.'

'Mmm, that's an idea. Otherwise we shall have to go.'

Pascale sniffed. 'Mario's just come in.'

'Oh, hell!'

'There's Mario,' Pete said to Nutty. 'The one in the red anorak.'

'Cor!'

'He's looking for Claudine.'

'Claudine's going! She's getting up.'

'She's avoiding Mario,' Pete said. 'It's like a chess-game.'

Claudine and Pascale had wriggled out from behind their table and started to dodge across the now filling dance-floor where couples were gyrating in exactly the same way as they did at the Northend Lido on Saturday nights. They came straight towards Pete's party and stood smiling down at them.

'May we join you?'

'Sure.' Pete turned round and hooked another chair away from the table alongside, and they all stood up and shoved round to allow the two girls to squeeze in. Hoomey, jerking awake, found himself looking straight into the incredible violet eyes of the most desired girl in the south of France.

'Vous-êtes fatigué? Already?'

His mouth dropped open.

41

At the same moment Mario Cellini, having shouldered his way rapidly across the bar, pushed past Pete and stood, flashing-eyed, before Claudine.

'Viens, cherie!'

Claudine did not move. She looked up at him from beneath the longest eyelashes Hoomey had ever seen and said, 'Je regrette, Mario . . . je vais danser avec Peregrine ici.'

Hoomey felt his hand taken gently between her warm, soft fingers. She stood up and pulled him firmly to his feet beside her.

'Il est Anglais. Son père est le proprietor de Harrods. Il s'appelle Peregrine Plunket-Masham-Blandford-Fitzpatrick. Voilà, Peregrine, mon vieux ami, Mario Cellini.'

She pushed his hand out firmly and placed it in the enormous hairy grip of Mario Cellini. Cellini ground it viciously, so that Hoomey nearly cried out.

'Enchanté, Peregrine,' he said.

'Maintenant, excusez-moi, Mario. Viens, Peregrine.'

She pulled Hoomey firmly out from behind the table and led him two steps to the dance-floor, where she put her arms round him and pressed him firmly to her delectable body.

'Dance with me!' she hissed urgently into his ear. 'As if you love me!'

If she had not held him so firmly, Hoomey thought he would faint. He stumbled helplessly into the throng, his eyes glazed with terror.

The others sat staring in amazement.

'*What* did she say?' Mark breathed.

'She said, "This is Peregrine Plunket-Masham-Blandford-Fitzpatrick. His father owns Harrods",' Pascale said in clear English. She spread open Claudine's copy of *Elle* at a page of photographs of London night-life. 'There.' She indicated with a long brown forefinger where there was a list of names containing the various ones Claudine had just bestowed on Hoomey. She smiled. 'It worked well. Look at Mario. He's furious.'

Mario was indeed staring into the dancing throng, clenching his hairy fingers angrily around his wineglass. He half-turned back to them, and glared at Pete.

Nutty, seizing her opportunity, stood up and placed herself squarely in front of him.

'Mr Cellini, my name is Deirdre McTavish, and my father owns the Albert Hall. Please will you dance with me?'

Mr Cellini made a sort of snort and stormed away back to the bar, leaving Nutty unabashed.

'That's no way to treat the customers,' she stated. 'I could be offended.'

'But you're not?' Pete and Potter were highly amused. Pete said, 'If you want to dance with a real ski instructor—'

He got up. Nutty grinned, thinking he meant himself, but he turned away and fought his way out of sight through the crush.

'You have got a nerve!' Mark said to Nutty. His eyes were riveted on Claudine who still had her arms round Hoomey and was gyrating with him, smiling into space over the top of his head. He thought she was the most beautiful girl he had ever seen. Her emerald green track-suit shimmered in the revolving lights and her long hair sparked gold and silver. She laid her cheek down on the top of Hoomey's spiky hair and whispered in his ear. Pascale was killing herself with the giggles.

'Zat leetle boy—his papa—'Arrods! Regardez Mario! Il est furieux!'

As she spoke Gerard came up to their table and presented a neat French bow.

'Deirdre McTavish?' The name sounded quite different with a French accent.

43

'C'est moi,' said Nutty.

'Vous voulez danser, mademoiselle?'

Gerard held out a hand to Nutty. At close quarters his face was that of a very handsome monkey, his eyes dark and smiling. Nutty got up from the table with an ecstatic smile.

'Enchantée, monsieur,' she murmured, and stepped into his arms.

As they disappeared on to the dance-floor, Pete came back nonchalantly to his glass of lemonade.

'All part of the service,' he said.

14

David Moore slipped away while these exchanges were taking place in Piggy's Bar, wanting his bed, longing for the next morning. He made his way back to the chalet, his feet crunching in the frozen snow. The sky was ablaze with stars. He did not hurry, savouring every moment. It was almost like dreaming, hard to realize that the longed-for journey had actually taken place, that he was five hundred miles from home. Certainly the air had never felt like this at home— cold, yes, but not this splintery-sharp cold, the cold of being fifteen hundred metres high in the mountains. He spun the walk out, enjoying being alone with his feelings. The others in the bar ... it was stupid, he thought, to waste time on what one could get at home in Northend on a Saturday night. The crunch of his boots in the snow, the rumbling and rushing of the mountain stream under the bridge ... there was nothing like that at home. He thought fleetingly of his little bantams ... God, he was *lucky*! To think how nearly he had missed it—would have, if Biddy hadn't given him that encouragement. She was right. It was true, however tough it might be later to pay Nutty back, he'd have it under his belt. Nothing would take it away. Seven days, and one of them nearly over already! He had to be alone, to think about it, get the last ounce of flavour from every passing minute.

The chalet was quiet, although the lights were on. He made his way to his room, and found that he'd left his small bag with his washing things in it in Jean's room under the eaves. She hadn't joined them in the expedition to Piggy's—he supposed she was in bed by now. He'd have to creep up there, all the same, try not to wake her.

He tapped very quietly on the door, and opened it.

The room was in darkness. It was very cold. The window was open and Jean was standing there in her pyjamas looking out. She turned round, startled.

'Hey, sorry. It's me, David. I left my toothbrush and things.'

'Put the light on.'

Jean looked embarrassed. She had the duvet wrapped round her, and her face was flushed and bright.

'I was just looking.'

David picked up his duffle-bag, and came over to the window.

'It's so marvellous,' Jean said.

A half-moon had risen and by its light the mountains were now shining above the village. The view from the little attic window was up the valley, not down over the river as from most of the other rooms, and the peaks on either side of the col above glittered under the swags of freezing snow like some vast theatrical backdrop. Accustomed to the tat of what passed for 'country' in their home territory, both Jean and David found it hard to take in.

'I can't believe—I keep thinking . . . I'm not really here.'

Jean shivered, and shut the window, and laughed. 'You'll think I'm stupid.'

'No, I don't.'

He didn't say so, but David thought she was the only sane one of the whole bunch.

'It'll be great tomorrow, going up there,' he said inadequately.

He went to the door. 'Get in bed and I'll turn the light out.'

'I'm lucky, having this place to myself.'

'Yeah.'

None of the others would have thought that. David switched off the light. 'Goodnight then.'

'Goodnight.'

David padded back happily to his still empty room and went to bed.

15

Their ski instructors were Pete, Potter and the scornful Pascale. She was slender as a twig in her skin-tight plum-coloured suit with white choker neck and woolly hat, goggles pushed up as she considered the motley collection before her.

'I weel 'ave 'eem.' She pointed her ski-stick at Jazz.

'That means me as well,' Hoomey said, determined not to be parted from his protector.

'Peregrine?' Pascale smiled indulgently. 'Bien. Le petit Peregrine.'

Everyone now called Hoomey Peregrine.

'Le petit lapin,' Pascale smiled.

'What's she say?' Hoomey said to Jazz.

'Little rabbit,' said Jazz, grinning.

The awful rabbit on the back of his ski-suit, having

been laboriously unpicked by Mrs Rossiter, now showed in darker pink against the rest of the suit. Hoomey thought people were laughing at him, although Jazz looked pretty weirdo too, with a pair of punk goggles pushed up over his turban. Having picked Jazz, Pascale was landed with the gang that went with him: Nutty and Sylvie, David and Jean. Mark and Nick wanted to be with her but were deflected on to the long-suffering Potter.

'But we've been before! We can ski!' Mark proclaimed hotly.

'Good,' said Potter. 'Pascale's for complete beginners.'

Jean opened her honest mouth to say that she had skied before, but David shut her up. 'Stay with us! Don't say anything. You don't want to go with that shower, do you?'

Jean did as she was told. 'It was ages ago. When I was little.'

All the same, it had rubbed off. She felt strangely at home on her skis, and moved with confidence. Hoomey discovered it felt nothing like standing on the carpet in the shop.

Pascale stood them in a row at the foot of the nursery slopes. The nursery slopes were just up from the chalet, very convenient, and consisted of short, gentle slopes served by several tow-ropes. Beside them was a sort of station where people were climbing into little four-seater 'bubbles' which hung from a cable, and which swung them up across the valley to the higher slopes. Those were proper skiers, Hoomey supposed, who were going to whizz all the way down from the top. Count him out. He was quite happy to be in the nursery. The sun was shining and the snow glared up at him, making him squint.

Learning to ski was, Hoomey quickly decided, Very Hard Work. Once aboard, it was like being nailed to the floorboards and taking them with you everywhere you went. Or rather, where they went, for Hoomey found he had very little control: half the time he found himself going downhill backwards, occasionally forwards, and sometimes one leg did one thing and the other another. None of the others seemed to be having as much trouble as he was.

Pascale shook her head over him as he disappeared over a hillock, going backwards at gathering speed.

'Le petit Peregrine—!' She appealed to Jazz, 'He ees not—you say—très "with it"?'

The way she said it, it sounded like a compliment.

'He always *thinks* he can't,' Jazz explained. 'Whatever it is, he thinks he can't. That's his trouble.'

"Ee need the psychiatreest. Ze 'ead-doctor.'

For himself, Jazz thought that skiing with Pascale was pretty nice. She taught them to walk uphill in herringbone style and, when it got steeper, by stepping up sideways. Once at the top, they then zoomed gently down across the slope—leaning forward as instructed, with knees bent, weight on the downhill ski, going faster when the skis were parallel, easing up when applying a little snow-plough action, pressing out with the heels. To Jazz, a natural athlete, the whole business was magic. He only fell down twice and was out of control hardly at all.

Nutty, as usual, wanted to go too fast and was out of control almost as much as Hoomey but, unlike Hoomey, she thrived on excitement, and struggled heroically to get things right. Not for her the coward's way out of throwing herself down in the snow, although she fell, cursing herself, about twenty times during the morning. She was up in a flash, straightening out the tangle of sticks and skis, and away again as fast as before, willing herself to get it right.

Pascale said she was too impetuous, but admired her spirit.

'Relax! Relax!' she called out.

'How the hell . . ?' Nutty wondered, biting her lip with concentration. She was bearing rapidly down on the unsuspecting, thrust-out behind of a dowager lady instructing a tot of three or four who was already coping better than its elders and betters.

'Excusez-moi!'

Horror! French expletives . . . total disaster, Pascale swooping in like a hawk to sort out the mêlée, pick up child, soothe grandma, disentangle Nutty. Jazz laughed so much he crossed his skis and fell over. Pascale scolded in delicious French.

'Come, I take you up ze mountain, out of ze way.'

They queued at the bubble-car station, showing their passes. It was rather like a railway station, the plastic 'bubbles', seating four, coming continuously down the mountain, round the conveyor and onto the platform where they halted momentarily, doors sliding open, to take up their passengers. Nutty, Hoomey, Jazz and Jean Woods shoved in together, placing their skis hurriedly in the holder outside the car. They did not stop long. The doors slid to, the bubble trundled out of the station and, with a great lurch, off its rails into space, hanging from a cable. The sensation was extraordinary. Effortlessly they were carried up the side of the mountain, swinging high above the snow-slopes and zigzagging skiers. The machinery hummed softly and the majestic scenery unfolded itself beyond the steamy windows, the dazzling snowslopes golding already in the afternoon sun, ice glittering on the topmost rocky crags.

Hoomey was petrified.

'We gotta ski all the way down!?'

'That's the idea, mate. Machinery up, skis down.' Jazz grinned.

'It's miles!'

'Kilometres,' Nutty corrected.

'There's a green run all the way down,' Jean said. 'Look on the map.'

Green runs were for beginners; blue were slightly harder, red for more advanced skiers and black for experts. But to Hoomey, the colours blurred . . . The bubble was approaching the station and he was getting in a sweat. They did not linger long and he was terrified he wouldn't get out in time and would get carried on up to the very top where only the experts went. So anxious to get out, he then forgot to take his skis from the holder on the outside of the bubble, and it was only by Pascale imperiously stopping the whole works that one of the station attendants was able to retrieve them. Everyone in the whole station was glaring at him for the hold-up, or so it seemed to Hoomey—he wanted to die. As they stumbled down the iron steps into the glaring snow-light he determined to break a leg on the way down.

They lined up in the crowd outside and put their skis on again. Even at this, Hoomey took twice as long as everyone else, then dropped a glove, stooped to pick it up and fell over. All the others were laughing.

'Come, we 'ave to start before it gets dark,' Pascale said to him. 'You keep right be'ind me, Peregrine. And everyone follow.'

This was different from skiing down the short nursery slopes in the valley, starting off on a wide, curving piste that ran away down the mountain as far as the eye could see. Far, far below the dark trees waited to receive them, and the windows of the chalets glittered in the sun. Skiers from higher up flashed past with a clatter of skis on ice and twisted down off the piste into the soft snow, disappearing in clouds of powder-spray towards the treeline, dropping like arrows from a bow. Hoomey's mouth was dry, petrified by their example.

'Come along, darleeng!' Pascale called.

Hoomey fixed his eyes on her guiding bottom, so elegantly moving off before him. His legs were trembling and his skis wouldn't move.

'Get a move on!' Nutty called from above.

'Relax, Peregrine! Enjoy eet! Let ze skis run, trust zem!'

Hoomey relaxed and fell over again.

Pascale came back, smiling gallantly.

'You others go on,' she called out. 'Wait by ze post down zere.'

She hauled Hoomey to his feet. 'Now, do ze snow-plough, face down ze 'eel. You go veree slowly, be'ind me.'

Hoomey started to inch down the slope, pressing desperately out with his heels. Little children and ancient old ladies flashed past him. Pascale could ski easily downhill while watching him right behind her, calling out encouraging words. It was like a dog-obedience class, Hoomey thought. And fell over. The others were waiting at the post.

'Oh, honestly, Hoomey, you can't really be as bad as that! You're pretending!' Nutty called out.

Even Pascale, glancing at her watch, seemed a little worried.

''E 'as to go now. 'E cannot go back. I weel look after 'eem. You others, go on carefully. Keep to ze green. Keep togezzer—zat is ze important theeng. Ze fastest wait for ze slowest.'

She turned to Hoomey sternly.

'Now, come, Peregrine. We 'aven't all day.'

It seemed he was stuck with Peregrine for ever. He launched himself off again and managed to fall and go a good long way on his back, which was fairly lucky, but after that progress was painfully slow, and his legs started to tremble so much he could hardly stand up. The others had whizzed off (relatively) and it wasn't until they were emerging on to the nursery slopes in

51

the last of the afternoon sun that they came across them again, filling in time by going up on the beginners' tows and skiing down, round and round. At the foot of the slopes stood old Sam on his crutches with Big Brenda beside him, having tottered out to see how they were getting on.

Hoomey, seeing that he only had one more gentle slope to conquer before blessed rest and home, felt the dreadful tension of fear and anxiety drain out of his body, and launched himself off for the bottom with— at last—a feeling akin to joy. It was, after all, the babiest of the baby slopes. He heard Pascale cheering him on—'Magnifique, Peregrine!' and felt the icy wind whistling past his cheeks as he gathered speed, trusting his skis at last, letting them run. For a moment or two he experienced the real bliss of skiing, the glorious exhilaration of effortless flight over the hissing snow, the ease of movement and the excite- ment of momentary speed . . . the golden light dazzled his eyes . . . faster, faster . . . Now he knew there was no stopping, he had no idea how, the snow-plough at this speed being beyond his most earnest endeavours. The exhilaration crescendoed into the most almighty fear.

'Excusez-moi!' he bellowed, as disaster loomed. Big Brenda's eyes out on stalks, Sam lifting his crutch as if to ward off the inevitable . . . the impact of padded bodies colliding, all breath punched clean away . . . Hoomey felt himself flying through the air, his skis sailing away in another direction entirely, along with Sam's crutches, and then the uncomfortable crunch of landing on ice and sliding, sliding . . . It was complete and total catastrophe. Hoomey shut his eyes and lay still, not wanting to know.

But nobody seemed to be bothering about him. When he half-opened one eye, cautiously, all the action was around Sam, who was sitting in the snow with his plastered leg stuck out in front of him, making gibbering sort of noises and clutching his arm. Big Brenda knelt in front of him and the two Spotty Boys seemed to have appeared out of the blue and were once more down on their knees doing their first-aid act, prodding and shaking their heads. Pascale stood over them with what looked like a flare of incredulity in her marvellous nostrils, and Jazz and Nutty and Jean were staring with their mouths open, not believing the truth of it.

'Your wrist is broken,' Hoomey heard Pete pronounce. 'Not much doubt about it. You must have put it out to save your fall.'

Hoomey shut his eyes again. He wanted to die. Sam's wrist—the wrong man again. He would gladly have Sam's troubles, the lucky beast, first a leg and now an arm, positively hogging all the injuries when he, Hoomey, would give his right arm for a fracture ... or a fracture for his right arm. Hoomey wept.

'Come on, Peregrine, nevair mind.'

As a small crowd helped Sam across to the road to wait for an ambulance, Pascale and the others came to collect him.

'Just like an Exocet,' Jazz said. 'Straight down the slope, homing in on old Sam—wham!'

'First a leg and now an arm—and he's never even got on skis yet!' Nutty wondered, and then she started to laugh.

Jazz looked at her and started to laugh too, and then Pascale joined in. Even Jean Woods was smiling, leaning nonchalantly on her ski-sticks.

'Poor Sam!'

They all fell about, tears streaming down their faces.

'Poor old Sam!'

But Hoomey's tears were for real.

'Come on, Hoomey, it wasn't your fault. You couldn't have done it if you'd tried, could you? You never meant it. You were going a bomb—come on, don't get upset!' Nutty pulled him firmly to his feet. Pascale brought his errant skis back, Jean had his sticks.

'Nevair mind, leetle Peregrine, it's the way, in skiing. It was not your fault. Let us go and find Claudine and go and 'ave ze 'ot chocolat, and you weel feel bettair.'

Hoomey allowed himself to be led away, crashing over the heaped snow in his awful boots. He could not see anything funny in what had happened. Nor would the others if it had been them. They were all buoyed up by the magnificence of coming all the way down their first run successfully and by the amazing feel of it; only Nutty had fallen, but she was like a bouncing rubber ball and back on her skis again in an instant. As Biddy had pointed out long ago, it was much easier than falling off a horse. If they all found it so easy, why didn't he?

'It is the tension, Peregrine. You do not relax. You do not trust ze skis to take you,' Pascale tried to explain.

But look what happened when he relaxed.

'Zat is called ze bad luck.' Pascale had an answer to everything. 'Did it not feel good, before you 'it 'im?'

Yes, save he knew he couldn't stop.

By this time they were in the gorgeous fug of the chocolate shop, with the espresso machine hissing and burbling just like back home, and the smell of hot doughnuts lacing the atmosphere. Claudine was sitting at the best table in a corner, behind a large magazine, and the proprietor, catching Pascale's eye, led them over, bustling lesser mortals out of the way. Their boots crashed and slithered over the wet floor and the delectable heat enfolded them like a great blanket.

Claudine put down her magazine and smiled at

54

Hoomey. He felt himself going crimson and trembly all over.

'Peregrine, cheri, 'ow was it, ze skiing?'

Pascale launched into a great speech, eyes sparkling, no doubt telling her friend just how hopeless he was, and all about breaking Sam's arm, but Claudine gestured Hoomey to come and sit next to her, and Hoomey started to feel quite a lot better. The waiter brought great mugs of frothing chocolate all round, and some stunning cakes, and he felt back in his element again, in the real world, warm and cosseted and safe. He leaned across to Nutty and spoke earnestly.

'Honestly, I haven't got to go again tomorrow, have I? You can see I'm no good. I'd rather die than try again.'

Nutty looked at him pityingly. 'It's fantastic, Hoomey. It's just magic. When it works, that is. You can't just pack it in already.'

'Why not? We're supposed to be here to enjoy ourselves aren't we? I can enjoy myself jolly well here without bothering about skiing. I hold you all up dreadfully.' A good, unselfish ploy. Nutty fell for it.

'Yes, you do rather. But you're bound to improve.'

'But so will you, quicker. So I'll still hold you up.'

Claudine put her hand over his and said, 'You can stay wiz me, cheri. Eh, Pascale?' She added something in French.

Pascale said, 'Perhaps 'e should go in anothair class. Ze uzzers are veree good. 'E 'old zem up.'

'I'll take heem, myself,' Claudine said. 'My pupeel! I make heem very good, very quick!'

'I say!' said Hoomey.

'That's a fantastic idea,' said Nutty. 'What about it, eh, Hoomey? The others'll all die of jealousy.'

Jazz was grinning all over his face. 'Jeez—I'm looking forward to seeing Mark's face when he finds out!'

'Really?' Hoomey was a bit nonplussed.

'I tell Mario I 'ave a job,' Claudine said to Pascale.

It was all agreed, without Hoomey having an opinion.

'I see you 'ere, nine o'clock, Peregrine.'

'Yeah, okay.'

He was finding it hard to keep his eyes open, the warmth seeping into his battered body, awash with hot chocolate. The others were not much livelier, half asleep in their chairs. Outside it was already dark. The two French girls got motherly and said they must go 'ome for 'ot baths, so they got reluctantly to their feet and out into the cold again.

At least Madame Dubois knew that her reputation, like that of all skiing chalets, depended on the quantity of hot bath water she could supply at the end of each day and there was no dearth on that score. The news of Hoomey's collision with Sam Sylvester had preceded him, and poor Sam's fresh injury was the source of endless amusement, with Hoomey the centre of the entertainment. The higher the excitement mounted, the more determined Hoomey became never to set foot on ski again. Even Claudine would not persuade him.

16

By the time dinner was ready Sam was back again from the clinic with his arm in plaster, sitting down wanly to fish fingers and chips with plenty of tomato sauce. All the tables were pushed together at the end of the dining-room nearest the kitchen, away from the end which jutted out over the river, and it was very cramped and squashy. Sam, flinching visibly as his hungry classes fought and scrambled for their food all round him, was no doubt thinking back to his high hopes of wild boar in red wine and peasant cassoulet, easing his plastered limbs as he prodded at his fish fingers.

'What you going to do all the week, sir?' someone asked him.

'There's no such thing as boredom,' Sam valiantly answered, at which Jazz's father leant over the table and said, 'I will take you out, Mr Sylvester. We will go on expeditions.'

Sam looked rather surprised, and Big Brenda looked furious.

'Where?' she asked.

Mr Singh spread his arms expansively and shrugged. 'Other places, for nice French meals, and culture.'

Sam sneaked a sideways flash of interest.

'But I won't be able to come,' Brenda said.

Mr Singh shrugged again. 'Unhappily, no. You have your duties. But I am free. Mr Sylvester will help me with my English.'

Mr Singh was engaged in enlarging his vocabulary, for which task he carried around a large book called a thesaurus which gave a lot of different words meaning the same thing. He now looked up 'travel', and said to Brenda, 'Mr Sylvester and I will rove, flit, migrate, emigrate, immigrate, ambulate, ramble, promenade—'

'He can't,' said Brenda. 'He can't promenade. How will you go?'

'In the coach, of course. We will drive.'

He flipped over the pages of his book sharply. 'We will drive, urge, hurtle, boom, thrust, charge, jostle, hustle, encounter, collide, clash—'

'Try another page,' Sam said.

Mr Singh turned over diligently. 'We will advance, proceed, progress, move forward, push on, gain ground. We will learn English better.' He smiled.

Sam looked relieved. 'In the coach?'

'Yes, in the coach.'

'That's a very good idea, sir,' said Hoomey earnestly. He could see that Sam looked a lot less miserable at the prospect. Hoomey wished fervently that he could be included. News had spread about his appointment with Claudine. Marky-Parky and Nicky-Picky cornered him in the loo and asked him unbelievingly whether it was true. He didn't know what to say.

'It's not my fault! She picks on me!'

They goggled at him. 'You meeting her tomorrow?'

'Um—er—Pascale made me. I'm no good at skiing—I hold them up. So Pascale's sort of—er—dumped me on Claudine.'

'Just you alone?'

'Um—er—yes, I think so.'

They goggled some more, then cut all his front hair off with a pair of nail scissors. He had never thought he was any oil painting anyway, but when they left him he wept all over again at the sight—a sort of spiky desert in the middle of his head, with long bits sticking up round the edge like weeds round a field of stubble.

The others all fell about when they saw him. They were getting changed to go out dancing. They had asked Mr Singh to look up dancing in his book, and were full of his alternatives.

'We are going oscillating, Hoomey! We are going to waggle, wiggle and wobble, not to mention totter, dodder, shamble, flounce, flop and curvet. How about it?'

'I can't!' he wailed. 'They've cut off my hair!'

'Hoomey has had his hair abbreviated, whittled down, pruned—'

'Rendered short, reduced—'

'Hacked, hewn—'

'Foreshortened!'

They were all screaming and jumping on the beds

and throwing clothes about. Nutty came and put an arm round him. She had an arm like a chimpanzee. 'I'll improve it for you. Honest. You'll look all right.'

She fetched a pair of scissors and attacked the edges of his crop, snipping earnestly. She had taken out her contact lenses and could not see very well.

'Holy Moses, Nutty, leave him alone!' Jazz said suddenly. 'He's nearly a skinhead!'

'Well, he's even,' she defended herself.

'Evenly bald,' said Preston, an honest boy.

Hoomey started to cry again. He wished desperately he was at home. David Moore shouted at the others suddenly, 'Clear out! If you're going dancing, blooming well go! Beggar off and leave us alone!'

They did so, still hooting and shrieking, leaving the bedroom a shambles.

David started to tidy up. 'Don't worry,' he said to Hoomey. 'You look all right. They're all raving jealous, that's all.'

'What of?'

'Claudine, you twit.'

'Oh, her.' He couldn't see it. But at least she was better than skiing. 'Do you like skiing?'

David, putting back pillows, could not begin to say how much he liked skiing. It was like Mr Singh's book again: it was fab, brill, out of this world, magic. But to Hoomey he said, 'It's okay, yes.'

'If I don't do it, I'll be less trouble. I hold you up.'

'It's just getting the hang of it. If you persevere—'

'It'll take more than a week.'

'It's amazing how fast it comes though. In one day, to think what we did—fantastic!'

He could not keep the wonder and devotion out of his voice. Hoomey began to think that the week was going to be terribly boring, with everyone except himself becoming addicted.

'The weather forecast's bad for tomorrow,' David

said. 'Just our luck. They say it's going to be a white-out.'

'Whatever's that?'

'Cloud, I suppose. You can't see a thing, just have to follow the poles. You can't see the ground, they say.'

Thank goodness for Claudine, Hoomey thought.

When they stumbled up towards the nursery slopes in the morning she was waiting for him at the bottom, looking stunning in a cream-coloured suit, her matching cream-coloured hair glittering with snow. For the weather forecast was correct. There was very little to be seen except a lot of whiteness, and visibility was about the width of an ordinary room. The machinery still whirred and the bubbles and chairs were launching themselves up out of the valley into complete invisibility. It was bitterly cold and flakes of snow came on the wind. Pascale was with Claudine, waiting for her class.

'Can we still ski, miss, or is it too bad?' Nutty asked anxiously.

'No, we go. Gerard is coming wiz us, 'is pupeels do not like ze wezair.'

She winked at Claudine and laughed. They all got the message that Gerard liked Pascale.

'Are you sure you do not come, Peregrine?' she asked Hoomey. 'Per'aps today you feel more brave?'

'No, I don't.' Even less, if the truth were known.

'Ah, well—we go. Gerard—'e wait at the top, 'e say. We go meet 'eem.'

She said something in French to Claudine and they both laughed.

'Come, Peregrine, we go for chocolat, eh?' Claudine turned to Hoomey as the others started to struggle through the snow towards the lift. 'Alors, we enjoy ourselves, you and me.'

Her stunning smile seemed to bring the sun out for a moment. Basking in her attention, Hoomey slithered beside her back to the road. On the way they passed the Spotty Boys coming up with their classes, including all the smart bunch, the Parkers and Nick Picton. Spotty Boy Pete stopped her and said, 'Hey, that's one of ours. Where are you taking him?'

'Home, darleeng. I borrow 'im.'

'He's supposed to be learning how to ski.'

'I teach 'eem, do not worry.'

'Teach him what though?'

''E is 'appy wiz me.'

'I'll say,' said Mark Parker. Hoomey stood like a dummy during this exchange, wishing life were not so complicated. He could feel waves of envy and lust emanating from Mark and Nick and Preston, in fact from all the males, and how could he explain he only wanted the protection, not the girl? He wasn't after girls, which was the reason Claudine had picked him out. Even he wasn't so daft he couldn't see that. They needed each other to lead their desired uneventful lives, couldn't everyone understand?

Obviously not, judging from their expressions.

Their ways parted and Hoomey made for Claudine's home, with deep misgivings, wondering whether he might be getting into something even more difficult than skiing.

17

When Pascale's party emerged from the lift station at the top of the green run, they were blinded by cold white mist and whirling snow. They could only see each other if they kept close, and could only feel the shape of the snowslope beneath their skis, for with their eyes it was impossible to see where snow gave way to air or air to snow. Gerard was waiting for them, grinning like an amiable monkey. He was very brown and had dark brown eyes and a mass of curly black hair; he was short and chunky and not given to posing like Mario Cellini.

'I only bring zem today because zey are very good, for ze begeeners,' Pascale said to Gerard. She looked slightly anxious. 'Eet is not good, zis wezzair.'

Nutty couldn't see what on earth they were going to do. When she got her skis on, she couldn't even see where was up and where was down, only tell by the feel.

'Do you know the way?' she asked Gerard.

'Of course I know the way! You follow me. We keep very close.'

It didn't look a bit like the brochure. If the travel firm had put a photo of this in people would have thought it was a printing mistake—a shortage of ink. Everything was just a blur. Passing skiers could be heard swishing past; muffled shouts and a scream or two came from both above and below, but there weren't many people out, not like the day before.

Gerard and Pascale lined them up. Pascale was going to take up the rear.

Gerard said, 'You keep ze knees bended all ze time. You cannot see ze bumps, you must let ze knees take ze shock. You must trust ze skis, you must look up, not down, and ski as if in a dream. You must relax, relax, like in a dream. Feel ze snow take you, do not be afraid. No tension, just easy, easy.'

He smiled his enormous monkey smile and glided away as if in a dream, the others all lurching off in a panic, frantic to keep the person ahead in sight. After the first horrific heebie-jeebies, Nutty suddenly discovered that trusting the skis and skiing in a dream was the only way possible, as there was absolutely nothing else to go on. It did not stop her falling over in a dream and, once, hitting a tree in a cream, but the sensation was extraordinary and magical. The angle Gerard took was very gentle and he stopped often as they made their shaky beginners' turns; how he knew the way Nutty could not imagine, as they only rarely saw a green post slide by, but presumably the experienced skiers knew by signs she was unaware of, for several went past them, their faces screwed up with what Nutty presumed was fear and the dreaded tension. It seemed that skiing was a sport where everyone went as fast as they dared, and then a bit faster than that. They were doing it already and had only been at it two days.

Gerard made them take it in turns to ski immediately behind him, copying what he did. With one's eyes on his gliding, agile silhouette against the snow, it seemed almost easy, a charmed descent. Jean Woods, having supposed she was not into boys, fell violently in love with Gerard from the moment he turned to watch her and said, 'You are amazing! You must 'ave skied before? Zis is not your first time?'

'I skied when I was tiny, I hardly remember it,' she replied.

'Several times? Not just ze once?'

'Yes, several times.'

And he smiled his ready smile over his shoulder, the dark eyes gleaming through his goggles. He moved as if the skis were a natural extension of his body; one could not imagine him without them; he was an animal at home on the mountainside, his movements graceful and assured as the chamois. Pascale had said that he also held the speed record for the local Downhill, beating the famed Mario Cellini three times out of five.

'Cellini is so big-'eaded,' Pascale had explained over chocolate the day before. 'But Gerard, 'e think nozzing of 'is skiing. 'E just laugh.'

Jean, gliding through the white-out behind Gerard, felt as if she was on a cloud both mentally and physically; she could never remember being so happy in her whole life. The feeling was so strong that she wanted to catch it to store away, she did not see how it could possibly last or even happen again, not in just this exact, ecstatic way, all bound up in the white mist with the figure of Gerard smiling at her over his shoulder, praising her, pleased with her. She skied down in a dream, just as he had advised, but it was a dream of exquisite emotions far and away beyond the tactical dream advised by Gerard.

When they were down, and taking their skis off outside the restaurant for a hot drink and a rest, Jean saw Pascale exchange looks of relief with Gerard, and Gerard said something in French, shaking his head, the gist of which Jean guessed was, 'That was a crazy thing to do, with such beginners!' She knew that Pascale had taken them up because she had arranged it beforehand with Gerard. But Jean was not jealous of Pascale; she knew her place, and only needed to adore Gerard, ask nothing in return. She followed the others into the noisy, steaming café still in her dream, and sat alone at a table in the window, looking out on to the white mist outside, holding on to the bliss. The others were squashed on another table; Gerard and Pascale had joined a group of instructors, and only David Moore came to join her, hesitantly asking permission.

'Of course!'

'I thought perhaps—you know—' He recognized her trance, he understood—not about Gerard perhaps—but about the physical joy she had experienced. About wanting to think about it on her own.

She smiled. He had miles more sense than all the rest.

'It was good, wasn't it? Did you enjoy it?'

'Magic.'

He smiled back, and they sipped at the hot chocolate in silence.

18

Claudine lived in a purpose-built block of luxury flats on the outskirts of Claribel. As she went in a doorkeeper opened the door and bowed to her and also to Hoomey, with a murmur of 'M'sieur.' Claudine led the way to the lift, waited for Hoomey to follow her and pressed the button for the top floor.

'Zere is no one in, do not worry, leetle Peregrine.'

Did he look worried? Yes, he very likely did. He was worried.

When they emerged from the lift Claudine opened a door with her key and led Hoomey into a room so luxurious that he had only ever seen its like in films. Two complete sides were windows, but there was absolutely nothing to be seen from them save the soft white mist and falling snow. No doubt in good weather the view was fabulous, but now the snow filled the room with a strange pearly light. It was carpeted in pale gold and the enormous cushioned seats that ran all round under the windows were upholstered in white, with gold and silver-grey cushions. It was purringly warm and cosy and seductive, with a huge black stove opposite the windows filled with glowing pine-logs which Claudine opened up and got blazing instantly with a turn of a button or two. Great bowls of white and yellow chrysanthemums stood on low tables at strategic points, along with shiny magazines of the *Vogue* and *Harpers and Queen* variety.

Petrified by the thick white carpet, Hoomey took his boots off, and Claudine brought him a pair of fur slippers. She skinned off her ski suit to reveal another stunning creation—puce tights and a long black jumper that came down to her knees—and went into the kitchen to make hot chocolate. She produced tins of dreamy cakes and cookies, all oozing cream and icing, and set platefuls down beside Hoomey. Hoomey stopped worrying and sank into the cushions with a sigh of heaven—this was definitely more his style; the holiday was taking on a different complexion altogether. Five days of this he could bear quite well.

'I like you 'ere. It suit me veree well. Mario, 'e come 'ere when 'e 'as no pupils, 'e come at lunch-time, at twelve midi, always 'e come—'e is a great—how you say?—I theenk bore. 'E want marry me. 'E want marry zis appartement, ze ski school, you understand? 'E say 'e lurve me, but 'e lurve only 'imself. You see. When 'e comes now, 'e find you. You nevair leave my side while 'e 'ere, you understand?'

'Umm. Yes. Okay.'

The prospect did not appeal overmuch, but with a box of delicious chocolate creams beside him and the jug of hot chocolate with marshmallows floating on the top arriving, steaming, on a tray before him, Hoomey decided he would just have to make the best of it.

'My muzzair, she come too, per'aps.' Claudine made a face and shrugged. 'She is—'ow you say?—old bag?'

It did not seem quite the right description for one's mother somehow, but Hoomey decided to let it go. Never having met her, he was in no position to judge.

'You want video?' Claudine asked. 'Records? We 'ave Engleesh records, American records, French records . . .'

She put on an old Rolling Stones record. Hoomey was the only person he knew who wasn't interested in records—the only records in his house were some of steam-trains going over Shap that belonged to his father—but he was quite agreeable to background noise, and lay on the sofa looking at *Vogue* while Claudine got out a portable sewing machine and started to make a dress of some sort. After a bit he watched a French video of 'Jaws' and Claudine brought coffee with a lot of cream on the top. In the middle of 'Jaws' a bell rang and Claudine made a face and said, 'It ees Mario, I sink.'

She opened the door and Mario came in. When he came through the door the effect was of a whole moutainside moving in, such was his outdoor presence; a strong cold blast of air, flecks of snow flying as he flung off his natty headband and goggles, the strapping, gleaming hulk of the man with his tooth-dazzle and eye-glitter, his shining brown curls and bright red and yellow ski-suit. Hoomey, as directed, sprang to Claudine's side.

Mario gave him a disgusted look and broke into a lot of French annoyance. Claudine laughed and shrugged and sat down at the end of one of the sofas, leaning on the arm. She patted the seat beside her and Hoomey nipped in before Mario, very sharp. Claudine prattled on in French, and Hoomey caught the word Peregrine several times, and once, he thought, 'Arrods. Mario perched himself on the arm of a chair opposite them, and glowered angrily. Hoomey did not have to understand French to know what he was thinking.

Apparently Claudine made it clear that Hoomey was a fixture for after a while Mario made a vicious-sounding speech, picked up his goggles, gloves and headband and departed.

Claudine was delighted. 'It work famous, n'est-ce pas? You come every day, Peregrine, and 'e see I 'ave another boy-friend. 'E will get tired, I sink.'

If that was all that was required of him, it seemed amazingly simple.

67

'I get ze lunch! You like ze smoke salmon? Ze chicken? Ze roas' bif?' Claudine was all action, tying on an apron.

The kitchen was super-modern, but made to look like an old French peasant kitchen, with lots of checked gingham and swags of onions hanging from the plastic beams. Hoomey sat at the table and Claudine gave him a bag of nuts which he was just demolishing when Claudine's 'muzzair' arrived. Hoomey heard the turn of the key in the lock and the rustle of parcels dropping; Claudine pulled a face and he got up to be polite. The 'old bag' turned out to be another stunning female who looked only about ten years older than Claudine herself, dressed in a white fur coat, with masses of blonde hair, bright blue eyes and unashamedly false eyelashes. She gave Hoomey a very hard and rather puzzled stare, and Claudine introduced him with the name she had used the night before in the bar, give or take a few of the Fitzherberts and Bashems.

'Son père est proprietor de 'Arrods, en Angleterre,' she tossed off casually. Hoomey had been hoping to be relieved of this worrying honour, and was not reassured by the immediate glint that came into Madame Berthier's eyes at the lie.

''Arrods? Vraiment?' She turned on a blazing smile and kissed Hoomey on both cheeks. A torrent of French ensued, which Claudine answered spasmodically. Hoomey took another handful of nuts.

Madame Berthier then went off to change, gathering up all her parcels and Claudine turned her attention back to the cooking. Hoomey looked on hopefully. Claudine gave him a slightly worried glance.

'She's asked you to dinner, wiz your parents,' she said.

'But I'm with the school, not with my parents.'

'Mmm . . . well, I said—' Claudine gave one of her Gallic shrugs. 'I am sorry, I said somesing about your parents, and she say you must all come to dinner.'

'We can't.'

'Ah, well, it is arranged.' Another shrug, a sudden mischievous smile. 'We find you ze parents, Peregrine. It is simple. I ask Pascale—she will find . . . ze place is full of ze English people. My muzzair she is—'ow you say, très snob? We joke 'er.'

Claudine, looking very cheerful, started to chop some onions with great zest.

Hoomey realized that Claudine was a very bored girl, and diversions like turning him into the heir of Harrods and setting him up with some make-believe parents was just a way of relieving the boredom. But for him, it was something different altogether. His feeling of contentment evaporated fairly fast, and by the time they went out again to meet the others at the end of the afternoon he was very apprehensive. Claudine was full of high spirits.

The others had been doing turns on the nursery slopes all afternoon and all had trembly legs and frozen noses. They met them back in the chalet, where Pascale had been invited for tea, and the Spotty Boys were back with all the others. Claudine came back too. No one could understand why Hoomey looked so miserable.

'What did you do all day?'

'Oh, she kept making me coffee, and there was dinner with steak and salad and icecream and meringues and chocolate creams, and we played records and watched videos.' Claudine was talking nineteen to the dozen with Pascale and they were laughing and shrieking over their mugs of tea, not taking any notice of the boys anxious to strike up a conversation. Mark Parker, overhearing Hoomey's gloomy recital, said with deep sarcasm, 'How boring!'

Nutty, more perceptive, said, 'What's wrong with that? What's the trouble, Hoomey? Wasn't it what you wanted?'

Hoomey told them what the trouble was.

They gazed at him stunned.

'You haven't got any parents!'

'We find him some!' Claudine laughed, rejoining the conversation. 'We make it up. It is joke! My muzzair—she always look for ze smart people. We play ze joke on 'er?'

The Spotty Boys thought it a great idea.

'Put old Mario in the shade, eh?'

'You 'ave to find some people, some of your English friends—they 'ave to pretend to be Mr and Mrs 'Arrods. We dress zem up, veree smart.'

'When is this dinner party?'

'Ze night of Thursday.'

'Oh, jeez, two days! Who do we know? All our friends are too young!'

Pete said, 'There's that resting actor who washes up at the Tarentaise. He's about the right age. Robin somebody—'

'He's only thirtyish.'

'If he's an actor though—'

'Yeah, they act it, don't they? An extra twenty years. Piece of cake. I'll go and look him out.'

'I can act!' Nutty cried. 'I can be his mother—'

'Oh, shut up, Nutty, this is serious. We want some one really smart. Sophisticated.'

'Big Brenda.'

'Don't be daft!'

Hoomey could not believe his bad luck—everyone taking the idea to heart. They were really working at it, Pete staring into space with furrowed brow trying to think of a suitable female, Potter checking with Madame Dubois where Robin worked, Pascale suggesting where they could find some smart clothes that Claudine's

70

mother would not recognize.

'Do not worry, Peregrine!' Claudine noticed his appalled expression. 'My muzzair do not speak English well. We deceive her very easy. It is only ze joke.'

'Your father speaks it like a native,' Pete said unhelpfully. 'Is he going to be there?'

'Of course. And a few uzzairs.'

Hoomey let out a moan.

At this point in the excitement Miss Knox stood up with a list in her hand and called for silence.

'The Ski School wants to know how many of us will be entering for the Slalom Competition on Friday—I just thought I'd check, now we have all our instructors present. Apparently they always make a course for the last day, and all the beginners have a go—a bit of fun for you all! Now Peter, how many in your party? Just let me have the names.'

She wrote them all down, then Potter's party, and then Pascale's.

Pascale omitted Hoomey's name.

Miss Knox frowned. 'We're one short, surely? Whose name isn't down?'

Mark Parker said unkindly, 'John Rossiter.'

'John, of course. He's with you, Pascale? Why didn't you say?'

Pascale made a wide Gallic shrug. 'I forget.' She made a face at Hoomey. Miss Knox wrote down his name and gave him a sweet smile.

'I'm sure you won't want to be left out, John. Show them what you can do, eh?'

Hoomey, having decided he was going to be too ill to get out of bed on Thursday, decided to prolong the illness to Friday as well. The week was getting to be a survival course of a most complicated nature.

'Is Mr Sylvester back yet? Has anyone seen him?'

No, nobody had. For thinking up this holiday and

getting him into this mess, Hoomey hoped the old coach had zoomed off the road and deposited Sam ten feet under a snowdrift. Which is just where he would rather be.

But half an hour later Sam and Mr Singh came back, Sam slightly unsteadier than his plastered leg allowed for, a dreamy smile on his face.

'We have been sampling the culture—the cuisine—the vin du pays—a most interesting tour of the local environment,' he said woozily.

It occurred to Hoomey, somewhat indignantly, that he might have done Sam a favour, giving him the chance to spend the week swanning around in the bus sampling local delights. More of the vin du pays, by the look of him, than the culture.

After their nightly feast of fish-fingers, chips, jelly and icecream, the Spotty Boys were dragging on their anoraks to go out on what was now known as Operation 'Arrods.

'You've got to come,' Jazz said to Hoomey, who wanted to go to bed with the pillow over his head. 'After all, it's your parents we've got to find.'

The others were all fighting to join in the fun, even Mark and Nick, as Claudine was leading the expedition. Pascale was coming too. They went out into the freezing night, and Hoomey gazed longingly at the glittering outline of the now deserted and clear mountain ridge above the village, wishing that he had stuck with skiing after all. It couldn't be worse than what he had got himself into.

Robin apparently worked in a rather smart restaurant washing up. He was what was known as a ski-bum which meant he would turn his hand to any job as long as it gave him a few hours a day skiing. He turned out to be a hollow-cheeked, bearded, bejeaned man of indeterminate age, looking less like a sleek proprietor of Harrods than anyone Hoomey could envisage. Over the washing-up, Claudine, Pete and Potter gave him an enthusiastic run-down of the adventure ahead, to which he nodded amicably and said, to Hoomey's horror, 'Sure, sounds great. Count on me.' Apparently the lure of the dinner itself was enough. 'I can change my night off—Thursday, you say. That's okay.' He also offered to produce a 'wife'. 'I know just the job. Forty if she's a day. Very hard up. We get paid for this as well?'

'You get paid, yes,' Claudine said, smiling.

'We ought to have a dress rehearsal,' Potter said. 'Get it right. How about you two coming round to the Clair Ciel tomorrow night and we'll see about kit and everything?'

'That dump not slid into the river yet? I thought it was unsafe?'

'For heaven's sake, shut up,' Pete said hastily. 'Want to lose us all a job? The builders are coming as soon as the weather lets up.'

Nobody but Hoomey seemed to take the proposed deception seriously—it was all just a big joke. Claudine, they said, had 'great ideas'. Claudine could do no wrong. Claudine, Hoomey could see, was using him. When he complained to Jazz all Jazz said was, 'Aren't you lucky she chose you, man?'

Nutty thought the same. Too young to be Mrs 'Arrods, she was now trying to get a job with Claudine to wash up on the night, so as not to miss the fun. Claudine was doubtful, but promised to see what she could do.

'It's great this place—fab holiday!' Nutty was saying.

Never a dull moment, Hoomey thought gloomily.

Betty Dubois was planning a party for the Friday night after the slalom competition, to give out the prizes and have a farewell dinner. Hoomey longed for this concluding ceremony, and the end of all his troubles.

19

The following day, which Hoomey spent at Claudine's getting briefed about his life-style—'I sink you go to zat school they call Eton, n'est-ce pas? It is ze school for ze rich people, I sink?'—the others spent on brilliant sunlit slopes practising their turns and being introduced to the sideslip.

'You can do ze sideslip—then you can go anywhere, even down ze steepest slope,' Pascale assured them.

The idea was to stand sideways on to the slope with the uphill edges of the skis digging in to keep one in place, then to tilt the skis gently over sideways until they stopped digging in and were flat on the snow. One then slid down broadside on to the slope until, by tilting the uphill edges into the snow again to brake, one came to a controlled stop.

That was the theory.

'It is ver' easy,' Pascale insisted.

Not so, thought Jazz. Everything looked very easy the way the experts did it. 'No problem!' they cried airily, flicking their skis round in perfect parallels— the ultimate perfection in skiing. Snowploughing was only for beginners. Already they were all ambitiously trying to turn keeping their skis parallel, not easy at all at this stage. The only person who could do it was Jean Woods. She was an intuitive skier; she could not explain how she did it.

'It must be because I did it when I was little,' she said, not wanting to be thought clever. She did not want to be noticed, only by Gerard. She was still skiing in a dream, a dream of love for Gerard. When he came to look for Pascale, joining them in a mountain café at midday or mid-morning, Jean could not keep her eyes off him. When he passed them on the slopes with his private pupils, raising a ski-stick in greeting as he hissed past, she knew her day was made. She dreamed of him winning the Downhill, the hero of all; she dreamed of winning the Slalom on Friday and his giving her the prize, taking her hand in his to shake it, looking into her eyes with his delectable smile . . .

When his name was mentioned and she turned scarlet, David grinned at her. He knew her secret. He couldn't get his sideslipping right. He went forwards all the time. She tried to help him but could not say why she was doing it right and he wasn't. Pascale swizzed down to the rescue.

'You 'ave your weight too back. You lean back. You must get ze weight more forward.'

With such an ambitious class she had her work cut out to keep them all together.

As the day progressed the sun was hazed over by thin cloud.

Pascale made a face. 'Ze forecast for tomorrow is bad. Lots of snow. But okay after.'

'We can ski though, miss, can't we? We did the other day?' Nutty could not bear the thought of missing anything.

'We see.'

When they met up with Hoomey again in the evening Nutty said to him, 'The forecast for tomorrow is bad.'

'You're telling me,' Hoomey said.

'Your parents are coming tonight,' Pete said. 'Sort of trial run. You've got to decide where you live and all that, so you all tell the same story. It's good, isn't it, like a sort of alibi? Setting up a deception. I reckon you could have a load of brothers and sisters—'

'Hey!'

'No, at home, I mean. So's you've got something to talk about.'

'Humphrey and Algernon—'

'And Virginia and Sophie—'

'And you go hunting with the Quorn and have tea at the Ritz and—and—' Their knowledge of the habits of the rich was slightly limited.

'Have a summer home in—in the Caribbean. What d'you know about the Caribbean, Hoomey?'

'Where is it?'

'It's in the Pacific.'

'It isn't.'

'Hoomey can choose. Where d'you want a summer home, Hoomey?'

'In Northend.'

'Don't be loony! Honest, if you could choose—'

'Leeds.' He had a grandad in Leeds.

'You've absolutely no imagination at all! You *could* enter into the spirit of the thing!' Nutty was furious with him. 'If it was me—I wish it was me!—I'd think up all sorts of things to tell 'em. I'd go to Roedean and we'd have racehorses and a Rolls Royce Corniche and—'

'Oh, shut up, Nutty, it's not you. You want to get your face in everything!'

Apparently the Spotty Boys had arranged for Robin and his 'wife' to come round to the chalet after supper.

'We've got to fix a name, for a start. What're they called, these 'Arrods people.'

Claudine's accent was catching.

'Plunket something,' Nutty said. 'Plunket-Masham-Fitzsomething—'

'No, we've got to have something you can get your tongue round.'

'Smith,' said Nutty.

'No, you fool!'

'Smythe then.'

'I can't say Smize,' Claudine said. 'Why Smize?'

'Peregrine Potter,' said Nutty. 'Peregrine Potter-Smythe.'

'Peregrine Podder-Smize,' said Claudine. 'Mistair and Missiz Podder-Smize.'

'Poddersmize. That's good,' said Nutty.

'It'll do.'

'Who does own 'Arrods, anyway?' Preston asked.

'A Scotsman, I thought,' said Mark.

'Macpoddersmize,' said Nutty.

'Mistair and Missiz Magpoddersmize.' said Claudine.

'That's okay.'

'They're here,' Pete said suddenly. 'Hey, look at that!'

In the noisy dining-room a surprised hush had fallen at the appearance of the couple in the doorway. Madame Dubois stopped with her icecream scoop in mid-air.

'Madame Dubois?'

The gentleman in evening dress looked round with a charming smile. 'Excusez-moi, madame, mais je cherche—'

'It's us,' said Potter, standing up, grinning. 'It's us you're cherching. Mate, blimey, I didn't recognize—!'

A pained expression crossed the gentleman's features.

'M'sieur?'

'That's really great! I never guessed—' Potter went over to the man and gave him a great biff of congratulation on the back. 'You look a right smartie, mate. Left the Rolls outside, eh? Just dropped in for a glass of champagne? That's terrific!'

He took the man's arm and turned to grin at Hoomey. 'How about it, Peregrine? How's your father, eh?'

The man, looking puzzled, said in an undeniably Harrods voice, 'I'm afraid I don't understand.'

'It's really great, man! Fantastic!'

Potter pulled the visitor over to the table where they were still all sitting. The extraordinarily regal-looking lady who was with him followed nervously.

'What a get-up! Where d'you borrow the outfit from then? It's got real class—cummerbund and all!'

He fingered the silk lapels appreciatively and then turned to Mrs Harrods admiringly. 'Jeez, those diamonds! You could kid me they're the real thing!'

He picked up the glittering chain and let it fall back with a thump on the lady's ample bosom. The lady's eyes spat sparks as bright as her jewels.

'What exactly do you think you are doing, young man?'

Potter stared admiringly. 'That's great, that's really great. The voice is bang on, and that upper-crust expression, like a camel—terrific!'

'Like a what?' the lady said.

'A bloody camel, gel, you look just like a bloody camel.'

'Potter, just a minute—' Jazz murmured.

Mrs Harrods was turning an exciting shade of beetroot. Mr Harrods' expression of benign goodwill was gradually faltering.

Jazz tapped on Potter's arm. 'I think you've got it wrong.'

Potter gaped at him. Simultaneously, the undeniable figure of the bearded Robin appeared in the doorway from the kitchen, looking exactly like himself, and said to the Spotty Boys, 'Sorry if I'm a bit late. The old lady—I mean Mrs Harrods—can't get down here for another hour. Then she's got to pick up her gear.'

Potter went white and made a sort of moan.

Mr Harrods said, 'We didn't come here to be

insulted! We came to ask someone to move a bus out of the way so that I can get my car to the door of my chalet and unpack my things. Do you usually talk to perfect strangers in this way, young man?'

He turned his gaze on Potter who seemed to wilt physically, as if a laser beam had got him. His mouth opened and shut several times like a goldfish, then he turned and scooted out of the room.

'I think, sir,' said Mr Singh, standing up and bowing deeply, 'that there has been a misunderstanding . . . a misconception, or should we say a miscalculation?'

Mr Harrods blinked.

'Or should we say we are barking up the wrong tree, without a leg to stand on?' Jazz whispered.

'I will move the bus, sir, at once. And your lady wife is not like camel, the boy mistake her for someone else. We apologize deeply.'

He bowed again.

The lady like a camel stared at him in disbelief.

'Come with me, please. I help you park car.'

He took her by the elbow and with the utmost courtesy escorted her back to the door. Everyone stared as the couple departed. There was a long, astonished silence.

'Whatever was all that about?' asked Big Brenda.

'Has Potter gone out of his mind?' Madame Dubois said to Pete. 'Has he gone stark, staring, raving mad?'

'No, just his usual self,' said Pete.

'He thought—' Nutty started to grin. How to explain? 'He thought they were friends of his, in fancy dress.'

Naturally Madame Dubois was none the wiser. 'The boy's an idiot. I've always known it. That must have been our new neighbour—the chalet next door's just been sold. Sir Somebody or Other Partington. His sons are mad on skiing. A splendid first introduction, I must say!'

They followed Potter out into the kitchen, and Robin gave him some medicinal brandy out of Madame Dubois's first aid cupboard, having heard about his boob. Everyone but Potter thought it fantastic—'You look just like a bloody camel, gel!' was a phrase he was not going to forget in a hurry. Hoomey was relieved someone else in the place besides himself had something to worry about, but nobody was giving him brandy for his miseries. For some reason, he was assumed to be lucky.

'Claudine's little lamb—what more do you want in this life?'

'Wining and dining with the smartest family in Claribel! You don't know you're born!'

They dressed him in the clothes Claudine had 'acquired'—silk shirt, cashmere sweater, grey flannel trousers, a silk cravat and Gucci shoes. Somehow, they all agreed, even in all the right gear, he still didn't seem to look like anybody save Hoomey, whereas Robin, in evening dress, shaved, and affecting a slight stoop of the shoulders as if burdened by the worries of running Harrods, looked like a completely different person. Everything about him, his voice, his demeanour, his way of moving, was quite different, utterly Harrods. Everyone was captivated by the transformation, full of admiration. But for Hoomey there was no such approbation.

'Jeez, Hoomey, you've got to look like you own Harrods! Not like some one who thinks he's just stood in a dog's mess.'

'I—'

'You've got to look like—like—'

But nobody knew what the Son of Harrods quite looked like.

'More—um—'

'Rich.'

'Pushy.'

'Stuck up.'

'Etonian.'

Hoomey thought you had to have a white collar and a top hat to look Etonian.

'It's an attitude,' Robin explained. 'You've got to feel confident and a touch arrogant, perhaps.'

But even he could see that Hoomey couldn't act confident and arrogant when all he wanted to do was die.

'Perhaps we could give him pills for it,' Pete suggested. 'You know, like you can take before an exam. People do, don't they?'

'That's tranquillizers. To stop worrying, you mean?'

'Yeah, that's it.'

The others looked doubtful. With Hoomey, you could never tell.

'He'd probably fall off his chair.'

His mother turned out to be a buxom blonde called Angela who, like Robin, could turn on both age and class without any apparent difficulty. The whole thing was steam-rollering ahead, whether he liked it or not. Claudine was enchanted.

'We 'ave wonderful time! What beeg joke! I sit you next to Mario, mon cher Peregrine, and you talk him how rich you are and I tell eem 'ow I love you. He will 'ate you, Peregrine. 'Is eyes, they will kill you, Peregrine! Alors, c'est l'idée magnifique!'

She laughed her delicious tinkling laugh, and Mark and Nick and Pete and Potter and Jazz and all the rest hung on her every amusing word while Hoomey wriggled his toes inside his Gucci shoes and wished he had stuck with skiing: death on the slopes would be far preferable to death from Mario's eyes over the Berthier haute cuisine whilst pretending to be a young Etonian, rich, pushy and stuck-up.

20

The weather forecast for Thursday was 'deteriorating as the day goes on, a deep depression arriving by evening'. You're telling me, Hoomey thought. The others were all agog to get another day's skiing in before the snow arrived and were up and away to catch the first lift up the mountain. Hoomey had to go out with them, to demonstrate his presence to Miss Knox, who seemed to have the idea he was not keen. She gave him an encouraging smile and told him to cheer up. He went into the lift station with the others and came back down the exit steps on the other side and went to meet Claudine in the café. He kept telling himself, like exams, another twenty-four hours and this desperate day would be behind him—then he remembered that another desperate day was waiting to take its turn, with the slalom race for a bit of jolly fun in the afternoon . . . a throat-burning pang of homesickness and self-pity almost engulfed him as he faced the rigours of cappuccino chocolate and hot croissants yet again in the café . . .

Meanwhile the others were pestering Pascale to let them do a long run down the mountain 'properly'.

'You are 'ere to learn,' she protested. 'First you must practise ze turns and ze sideslip. All morning. Zen zis afternoon, perhaps, down ze mountain.'

'But the weather's closing in this afternoon,' Nutty pointed out. 'Can't we do it first, and the lessons later?'

'Certainly not! You 'ave ze lessons first. It is ze rule.'

The sky had a brassy tinge, with thin cloud furring

the sun and a cold wind skittering across the slopes. It looked ominous.

'Suppose we can't ski later?'

It was in the minds of all of them: the terrible stories of people who went for a skiing week and lost half of it because of bad weather, even all of it! The thought of losing a moment was dreadful, the days flying by. Nutty had the most to say about it, but Jean and David, although silent, were both in an agony of fear that they might miss some precious skiing time. As the morning went on the cloud became thicker, obliterating the sun, and coming down low over the distant mountains. The wind was so cold they were all glad to get into one of the mountain restaurants at lunchtime, into the steamy warmth of massed bodies. To Jean's great disappointment Gerard wasn't there. Only two more days, and today he was missing.

''E go over mountain today, wiz a party,' Pascale said. ''E will be late back.'

She wouldn't see him, even later. The day looked greyer still, and Jean could not get interested in the great entertainment later in the evening—the Hoomey fiasco at Claudine's. Nutty was still trying to work out how she could wangle an attendance, but the prospects were not encouraging.

After lunch they went down the mountain from the middle station and did so well that Pascale decided that there was time to do it again. Just. They caught the bubbles back up again, and emerged in a near white-out on to the slope again. It wasn't as bad as it had been the first time, with Gerard, but more patchy, the snow holding off, but the cloud very low and dark. Although it was only three o'clock the afternoon seemed to have become dusk already.

'Come on, we waste no time,' Pascale ordered them. 'I go first, and you, Jean, take up ze rear.'

This was a position of privilege, meaning she was

the best. David went just in front of her. Jean thought, 'I am going to enjoy this. Relax, and just enjoy it, not try and do anything clever.'

Pascale set off, her class looping behind her. There were not many people about, and those that were went past at great speed. Jean loved to hear the wicked hiss of speeding skis as they cut across the snow like swords; she wanted to get left behind so that she would have room below her to see how fast she could go—no good doing it so close that she ran past the others— Pascale would scream at her and the others would think she was showing off. David fell and his ski came off. Jean went to help him retrieve it, and was glad of the opportunity. They were effectively left behind, and with luck Pascale would not look back too soon and notice. The weather was closing in fast and, in fact, by the time David was back on both skis again, Jean had lost sight of their party. But she could see the next pole at the side of the piste and knew there was nothing to be afraid of. There was a couple below them, one in a red jacket and one in a blue, the same as herself and David; with luck, Pascale would think it was them and not wait.

'You go first,' she said to David. 'I'm going to wait until you're nearly out of sight and then follow. I want to try something out. I'll catch you up.'

'Okay.'

She wanted to use the whole width of the piste, sweep down and then turn with some speed up, not do the pootling short turns that Pascale wanted them to do. She turned away from David and headed down the fall line as close as she dared, feeling her blood start to tingle as the skis gathered speed. How soon before she turned? She did not want to spoil this gorgeous descent, her confidence swelling with every second as she felt her balance perfected, her two skis travelling in miraculous unison, her body apparently weightless as she sped down the snowslope. Her eyes watered in the bitter wind and she could see nothing, only the ice-smooth snow beneath her. Never had she experienced such utter bliss. A mix of plain fear, exhilaration and pride flooded her with near ecstasy; she had never come within a million miles of such a feeling in all her span of fourteen years and she was going to hold on to it for ever . . .

Ahead of her the smooth piste gave way to a bank of soft snow. She pointed her ski-stick, sprang up from her knees and made a perfect turn, carving a rounded bite out of the snow so that it sprayed up behind her and she heard the faint rattle of its frozen flakes spewing out from under the skis. Then, swooping back down the icy piste, she was running faster and faster, knew she must turn again to avoid disaster or turn into the slope, but wanted to do neither. She saw David looming through the mist, having just turned on the far side of the piste, and aimed to pass directly ahead of him and turn when she was clear. But David, glancing up, saw her coming and panicked, lost his balance and was suddenly right in her path. She was on unavoidable collision course, and caught David from behind, propelling him violently forward. She saw the pole marking the edge of the piste—in fact, they caught it as they went, knocking it sideways, and then there was a void, nothing.

They fell together. How far, Jean had no idea, but it seemed to last a very long time, long enough for the mind to stand amazed, and very frightened, and to remember her mother and her home and all the comfortable things she thought in those seconds she would never see again. They were falling through space, not down the snowslope, the white mist enveloping them. If it were rocks below . . . the thought flicked through her mind; she knew real fear as she had never experienced in her life before, not the self-induced fear of a few minutes earlier when she had actually had her life comparatively under control, but the true fear of thinking death was at hand.

But they landed in deep snow. The moment of impact was confused, a sudden floundering instead of falling, snow in the mouth, skidding and rolling helplessly, a tangle of sensations—mostly relief because nothing was hurting yet. It all seemed to take an age. Jean could not believe her luck and, when she lay still at last, she was not frightened of what had happened, but only thanked God she was still alive. She could feel her heart thudding, her pulse racing, breath half-sobbing into the freezing snow. But the sky was still above, falling snowflakes looking black against the white cloud; the ground was firm beneath her, and in a few moments she was able to sit up and take stock.

'David?'

Her voice sounded thin and quavery.

She cleared her throat.

'David!'

He was below her, sitting in the snow as if he was about to eat his sandwiches. He was grinning as he turned round.

'Cor!' he said.

'Are you all right?'

'I think so.'

Jean tried to get up. Amazingly, she still had her skis on, which made it difficult. This was no ironed-out piste they were on, but deep virgin snow. A loose ski was sticking out of the snow nearby, presumably David's.

'Have you got a ski on?' she asked. 'Or none at all?'

'One's still on.'

'That's your other then, up there. I'll fetch it.'

Not to have lost their skis was a stroke of luck. She reached out for the loose ski and took it down to

David, who put it on. They then stood side by side, not knowing what to do next.

'Nobody saw us go, that's the trouble,' Jean said uncertainly.

They were on a steep slope which fell down into a white-out below them. There was nothing to be seen in any direction, only the marks of their fall above them, which even now were beginning to be covered by the falling snow.

'What we'd like to do is get back up on to the piste,' Jean said, 'but I don't think we stand a chance. We fell an awful long way by the feel of it.'

'Down must be easier,' David agreed.

But there were no comforting posts to guide them, no signboards to say there was a way down, nothing save soft snow disappearing into the mist.

'We ought to shout, perhaps,' David suggested.

It seemed silly somehow. They did make a few tentative noises, not really wanting to shout 'Help!'— it seemed too dramatic—but in fact, as the minutes slipped away and they realized that it was rapidly starting to go dusk, it occurred to them that help was, in fact, just what they needed. But by the time they had reached this decision and shouted in earnest, it was too late. The last skiers above had left the slopes, and there was not a sound to be heard in any direction nor a light to be seen, only the softly falling snowflakes steadily obliterating all signs of their passage. If anyone came to look for them, in a very short time there would be no signs at all of their fall. From merely feeling awful fools and sorry to cause worry to the others, they began to realize that the situation was really rather serious. Standing there in the deep snow they were already getting very cold. From being thankful and joyful at having survived the terrifying fall, they were backsliding once more into fear, the survival now not being quite so certain after all.

'What do we do now?' David said, after their last calls had echoed into the muffled air and only silence remained.

'My father knew all about this sort of thing,' Jean remembered. The thought soothed her considerably. Her father wouldn't have been afraid in their situation. At least, with dark falling and the cold increasing, there was no fear of avalanches—they only occurred when the snow started to thaw, not when it froze again at the end of the day. With luck they could find their way down—at least, if they could see which way to go.

'When the others get to the bottom and find we're missing,' David said, 'they're bound to send out a search-party if we don't turn up. Don't you think we should stay where we are?'

'We could dig a snow-hole, out of the wind,' Jean said.

She then remembered something she had discovered when she had zipped her ski pass into the inside pocket of her father's old duvet jacket. In the pocket was a survival bag made of silver foil. It folded almost to nothing and she could easily have remained ignorant of it, save for groping inside the pocket for the pass.

She told David, fishing it out.

'What do you think? If we try and make a hole, and get in this, it might see us through until a search-party comes? The alternative is to try and get down, but unless it clears, we can't see where on earth to go.'

'There might be another drop the same as we've just come over.'

'If the weather clears—you never know, there might be another piste quite close below us.'

'There's just about a full moon, if the snow stops. Have you got a map?'

They had all been given maps on the first day. David found his amongst some chocolate wrappers and biscuit crumbs in one of his pockets, but it was too dark already to see much, apart from which they did not know whereabouts they had come off the piste. They could see the piste they had been on, but in the conditions had no idea how far down they had been.

'We might not be far away at all—from civilization, I mean.'

'In that case, it shouldn't be long before we're discovered.'

They decided to try and dig a wind-shelter in the snow. It was imperative not to lose their skis, so they took them off and stuck them hard in the snow as if they were merely going into a mountain restaurant. Hands were the only thing to dig with, so they started burrowing away, glad to get the circulation moving again. Down and in, trying to keep a sort of roof . . . they stamped the floor down with their boots, compressing the snow, both of them very businesslike, and trying very hard indeed not to suspect that they were in as bad trouble as they rather thought they were. Funny, Jean was thinking, if this had to happen, she would rather be in trouble with David than with any of the others. He was stolid and sensible. Whatever he was thinking, he made no word of complaint, blame or apprehension.

Luckily the slope they had fallen on to was relatively sheltered from the wind, the snow blowing from the top of the ridge they had come from. By the time they had hit rock at the back of their cave, they reckoned they had made a reasonable shelter, although it was hard to keep a roof over it—it kept falling in. But it had decent sides, and they built up the front to try and make it igloo-like, so that any warmth they generated would stay around. All this took them a very long time and kept their minds off the danger they were in. It also got them very warm, as well as exhausted. David insisted that they work at a steady pace in order not to get too sweaty. 'If we get in a muck sweat, it'll be horrid when we stop,' he pointed out.

It was going to be horrid anyway, Jean thought. Waiting in the pitch dark with the temperature well below zero . . . she pulled out the survival bag and opened it out. They were certainly going to have to snuggle together: it wasn't very wide.

'Best to sit down and put our feet in first,' David suggested.

'What about our boots? Perhaps we should take them off?'

'We could sit on them, insulate our bums,' David said.

'We could put our skis underneath us.'

It had its funny side, making this unlikely nest, but making the very best of the situation was deadly serious. Pressed tightly together, they got the bag up around their bodies and over their heads, and managed to sit down on their boots. David had propped the skis behind them, to keep their backs off the rocks which might tear the bag, so they leant on them and found it, initially, not too uncomfortable.

'It's called togetherness,' David said.

Jean could not speak. They had done well, but she knew their situation was very serious. She had been brought up with an awareness of how to survive in the mountains, knew they had done all the right things. The survival bag gave them a chance. But how far was the temperature going to drop, if no one found them? Already, the action over, she could feel her body cooling off fast. They had no food at all, and the thought of a hot cup of coffee was persistent and painful. There was absolutely nothing to be seen save the nearest snowflakes fluttering palely before their eyes. The night was black as pitch and utterly silent. For all they strained their ears for any faint echo of sound—of voices, the church bell below, the engine of a pistebasher—they heard nothing but the murmur of their own breathing. They were quite alone on the mountain.

'At least, they know we're missing,' David said. 'We know they're going to look for us.'

'In this weather?'

'It might improve.'

'Yes. If only we could see . . . there might be a piste just below us.'

'We've got our skis, at least.'

What else to say? Jean thought of her father, his brown mountaineer's face, his very blue eyes with white lines round them where he had screwed them up against the sun. Already he seemed to her very young to have been her father; he had been just thirty-two when he died. She would never see him old and paunchy and cantankerous, but eternally a young man—there was something comforting and beautiful in this thought. He felt very close, or was it just her imagination? If anyone knew how to get out of the difficulty she was in at this moment, it was her father. If she held on to his memory, held his face fast in her mind, he would see her through.

21

The others waited in the hot chocolate shop. Pascale was worried.

'I thought zey would be waiting.'

'They're the best. They'll be down already. Perhaps they went straight back to Claridges.'

'I go look.'

'No, have a drink first. Claudine's here.'

Claudine was sitting in her usual corner, waiting for them. She was alone.

'Where's Peregrine?' asked Jazz, grinning.

'Oh, 'e go back to the chalet. 'E very—how you say—'

'Chicken! He's not flunking out?'

'Oh, no, I will not let 'im! If 'e do not come, I go fetch 'im.'

'Don't worry, we'll deliver him. We'll make sure he's here.'

'Mario is coming. I sit zem togezzer. I sit Peregrine between me and Mario.'

Nutty looked amused. 'Poor bloody Hoomey! Have you told him?'

'No. 'E won't speak wiz me.'

'Never mind, we'll give him a pep talk. We'll fix him.'

Claudine said something to Pascale in French. Pascale was silent and worried.

'I lose two of them,' she said. 'They are not here! I cannot stay. I must go look.'

'Honest, Pascale, they'll be at home.'

'Then I go look there first.'

'I'll come with you,' Jazz said.

Jazz thought it was pretty serious, a guide losing half its party. No doubt there were guides' rules about such things. Pascale looked close to tears.

'Come on, they'll be all right,' he said. 'They're the only sensible ones of the whole lot.'

'I looked back. I saw ze red jacket and ze blue jacket. I thought it was zem. Per'aps it was some one other.'

They went outside. Beyond the bright lights of the little town, the darkness was intense; no stars showed and snow was falling heavily. Suppose they were still up there, Jazz thought? Nothing seemed lonelier to his imagination than the high snow-pistes when the last of the skiers had gone down, the last lift had swung away towards the valley and the mountains had returned to silence and darkness. No, they must have come down, nothing could have gone wrong.

But they weren't back at the chalet. No one had seen them.

Pascale's face was drawn and taut.

'I go back—I find Gerard! I tell the Rescue!'

'What is it? What's wrong?' Miss Knox came into the chalet, stamping the snow off her boots in the doorway. Jazz explained.

'Pascale is going back—'

'I will come with you! Just let me change my boots.' Miss Knox was quick and businesslike. 'You stay here, Jaswant, and don't make it into a big drama—I'm sure we'll find them. Tell Mr Sylvester when he comes in, that's all. The bus isn't back yet.'

'Yes, Miss Knox.'

Jazz wanted to go back with Pascale. She looked terrible.

'Honestly, they're terribly sensible,' he told her. 'Not like the rest of us. They won't get into trouble.'

'If there's been an accident—it's my fault. It's all my fault!'

'Don't! It'll be okay, you see.'

There wasn't much he could say and, having been ordered to stay behind, he went up to his room to find Hoomey. .

Hoomey was lying on the bed eating a Mars bar.

'I'm not going,' he said. 'No one can make me.'

'You can't let Claudine down! What about Robin and that friend of his—you can't let them down—it's not on, Hoomey!'

'They can go out to dinner without their flaming Peregrine, can't they?'

'No. You've got to fend off Mario, for Claudine.'

'He's not coming, is he?'

'Yes, that's the whole point. Claudine really needs you.'

'She's just doing it for a joke, because she's bored rigid. She's just making a fool of me!'

'Oh, come off it, Hoomey, you can't take all that hospitality and be her friend and all that, and then opt out! She's not making a fool of you! She's making a fool of Mario, who's a real wally. You can see that for yourself. You've skived off skiing, you twit—you can't skive off this as well. You'll never live it down. What d'you think Mark and Nick and them'll think? If you do it—if you come home and tell the tale they'll be steaming jealous, Hoomey—just think of it—but if you don't go, you'll never be able to live with yourself—they'll really despise you. Everyone will, letting down Claudine after all she's done for you.'

Hoomey always believed everything Jazz said, and this loony spiel seemed to work, for Hoomey's expression dropped back into ineffable gloom.

'Okay. I'll go then.'

'That's a boy! Take your mind off it.'

'Off what?'

'There's worse things happening, mate, than your spot of bother. David and Jean have gone missing.'

'Missing where?'

'If we knew where, they wouldn't be missing. Last seen high up on the mountain. I've got to go and tell Sam. He's just come back.'

He could see the bus out of the window, manoeuvring into a tactful place to leave an opening for Sir Whosit's Rolls Royce. He ran down to meet Sam, whose happy smile was quickly obliterated by the news.

'Miss Knox has gone with Pascale, sir, up to the Rescue, or whatever. I don't think there's any need for you to go. Miss Knox said not to make a big drama of it down here—I mean, they've probably turned up by now.'

'I hope you're right, lad! Oh, my word, what a terrible worry.'

He had gone, quite understandably, pale with shock.

'But I've no doubt they have emergency action for this sort of thing. It must have happened before! Whatever were they doing?—the last pair I would expect to get into trouble!'

Jazz explained, and they went into the dining-room, where the other returning parties wanted to know if the rumour was true. Jazz played it down but the usual high humour and spirited fighting for the first baths was much clouded over by a general tension. Big Brenda came home and went out again to find out what was happening. When she came home she reported that a search-party was setting out to search the piste that David and Jean had last been seen on, led by Gerard. To Hoomey's bitter disappointment, Mario Cellini was not a member of the Rescue team and had not offered his services.

'If they stay missing, surely I can't go to Claudine's?'

'Look, you're bound to—they think you're Master Harrods—nothing to do with a school-party. You don't think everything grinds to a halt, do you, when there's a bit of a hiccup? Nobody's going to cancel their dinner-parties or anything. You've got to go in an hour—seven-thirty, didn't they say?—and the search-party will hardly have got started by then. By the time you come home, they'll be back in bed, bet you.'

Nutty joined in.

'Come on, get your gear on. Robin and Angela will call for you and you'll still be looking like a wally from Hawkwood, instead of a young Etonian.'

Realizing that nothing was going to deliver him, Hoomey got into his cashmere effort and, bang on the dot, Robin and Angela drew up outside the chalet in a smart Mercedes, calling for him with an imperious blast on the horn. Jazz and Nutty, Mark, Nick, Preston and Sylvie, all trailed out with him to make sure he got in.

'Where d'you get this job from?' Jazz asked Robin admiringly. 'Is it legal?'

'Yes, friend of Claudine's. She arranged it.'

A whiff of expensive perfume and heady aftershave floated from the open window. Hoomey got in the back. The others all lined up to wave him off. Nutty watched the departure with an expression of utter longing on her face.

'If only it had been me—Miss Harrods! I'd have done anything to have Hoomey's job—what a lark! He really is the boringest boy in the world, old Hoomey. Just fancy—' Words failed her, that Hoomey could not take the ownership of Harrods in his stride.

'At least he won't have time to think about . . .' Sylvie shrugged. 'Not with all that on his mind.'

'Think about what?' Nutty spoke, then remembered. 'Oh—them—they'll be all right. If it was me—'

She was off again. The others shoved her into a pile of snow and went back indoors for their supper.

22

'What do you think the time is?'

David had a watch on, but in the darkness they could not read the face.

'How long do you think we've sat here?'

David considered. 'An hour, perhaps.'

'Is that all? I think longer.'

'It certainly feels longer. But it's bound to, isn't it?'

'At least they'll know we're missing now.'

'Yes, they'll know all right.'

What they could do about it, given the conditions, David wasn't sure. They were both extremely cold and uncomfortable. It was difficult to move, cocooned together as they were by the bag, and the cramps were terrible. The boots beneath them and the skis behind them, although insulating them from the snow, felt as if they were made of knives. Cold was relative, David supposed. He was terribly cold, but he knew they weren't yet frostbitten, and with the bag over their heads, breathing down into the envelope around them, he thought they were keeping ultimate disaster at bay. So far . . . The night had scarcely started and was bound to get far colder. They said the hours just before dawn were the sharpest—certainly, in his experience, they were at home. They were out of the wind at least. They could hear it roaring off the ridge above their heads, but the side of the mountain they were on, by great good fortune, was in the lee.

'People sleep like this,' Jean said suddenly.

'What do you mean?'

'Climbers. My father has. When you're climbing and darkness falls, you just tie yourself on to a rock and sit there all night until it gets light again. It's like this, I suppose.'

'But that must be in the summer?'

'People do it in the winter too.'

'You mean, what we're doing is what climbers do quite often?'

'In a way, yes. But they're prepared. They've got food and a stove and make tea and that.'

She wished immediately she hadn't said that; the mental picture of a hot kettle and a brew of tea was tantalizing in the extreme. They had kept real thirst at bay with snow, but snow was horrible to eat.

'These bags—it's what they're for. They're supposed to keep the heat in and see you through.'

97

David considered.

'You're not frightened?' he asked tentatively.

'Are you?'

'I'm not sure. It depends . . . if the weather clears, or gets worse . . . it depends on how long, I suppose.'

'I'm frightened,' Jean said. 'But also—sort of—excited—'

'Excited how?'

'Well, I know it's gone wrong, but what we're doing—I mean, being here, in these mountains, what we've done this week—it's been fantastic. It's as if—as if you've come alive, properly—I never knew it could feel—I don't know how to say it—I can't. But suppose we hadn't come — we'd never have known . . .'

David, in the darkness, actually smiled.

'I know what you mean. Some wouldn't,' he added.

'It all makes sense, with my father. I understand now. I never did before.'

'Understand what?'

'My father was a climber. Mountains were his life. He had to be in the mountains. If he was at home for more than—say—six months—well, he never was. He couldn't stay.'

'My father's never left home that I know of, save to go into Northend, or the market in Helmsford. I don't think he's ever even been to London—not that I know of.' David spoke with deep scorn. 'You might as well be dead,' he said.

'My father went to the Himalayas, and to the Andes, and here—the Alps—all the time.'

'Why? What did he do?'

'He was a climber.'

'How do you make a living, climbing?'

'You take parties—guide people, teach people. But usually we were short of money, because he went off on his own.'

Jean hoped David wouldn't ask what had happened

to her father, and he didn't, as he knew already.

Jean thought that her curious lack of fear, considering the circumstances, was something to do with her father. She felt very much that he was close to her, and if she trusted herself to his spirit, she would come through. She would not dare admit this to David, but it was what had prompted her to talk about her father. In the last few days she had come to understand everything about her father—or so it felt. He no longer was the unfathomable half-stranger who had come and gone in her childhood, but someone with whom she was now truly flesh and blood. She understood exactly what had driven him and, in those few moments before the accident, she had discovered something about herself, about life, about her father, that made more sense than anything else she had ever come across. It was not the moment to die—when she had made this momentous discovery. A great shiver ran through her and her teeth started to chatter.

'It'll be okay,' David said, feeling it. 'They'll have to find us—frightfully bad image for the resort if you lose your clients. Claudine's dad would never allow it.'

A feeble enough remark, but comforting and kind.

'I'm glad it's you I knocked over. Imagine sitting here with any of the others—Nutty, for instance.'

'She couldn't sit still this long.'

'Jazz would be okay. The only one.'

'Hoomey'll be at his dinner-party now.'

It was hard to believe that somewhere below them, not even very far away, the village was continuing as usual, the bright lights glittering and the restaurants and bars crowded with skiers safely home from the slopes. The raging wind and thickly-falling snow would merely add to the atmosphere, make the warm and fragrant indoors more attractive, the hot bath more delicious.

The searchers on the piste above them searched in

vain, their shouts and cries carried off the mountain by the high wind, far out of earshot of the two who crouched in their inadequate snowhole. The darkness was absolute, the steadily-falling snow beginning to pile up around them and over them. The faint warmth of each other's body was the only small comfort as the slow hours passed, and fitful dozing a frightening intimation of the ultimate unconsciousness against which they both felt they must fight. There was a limit to their powers of resistance and, if the weather did not relent, David did not think, in his heart, that they would survive the cold dawn.

Strangely, he thought of his little bantams. If it hadn't been for them, he would never have come. But, even more strangely, he regretted nothing. He started to tell Jean about his bantams, describing them one by one, and if she thought he was losing his mind, it was better than sitting in silence listening to the far wailing of the wind and the occasional mutterings and grindings of invisible rocks in the river far below.

23

'Ah, mon cher Peregrine!'

Madame Berthier descended upon Hoomey in a cloud of scent, feathers and curls to give him an almighty kiss on either cheek. She was smellier by far than his parents, almost as fragrant as Mario Cellini, who was already eyeing him in smouldering fashion from across the room, dressed in the most expensive of casual après-ski gear, teeth a-glitter as usual. Why on earth Claudine could not fall in love with this beautiful man Hoomey could not for the life of him fathom. Mario advanced to be introduced to Robin and Angela who looked as if they attended dinner parties such as this every night of the week. Hoomey in fact knew they were starving, for they had remarked upon it in the car, and hoped their piteously empty stomachs would not roll too loudly before the off. Claudine's father was talking to another couple in front of the roaring stove, and turned to greet the newcomers. He was a tall handsome man of flinty charm, not, Hoomey thought, the sort of man who looked as if he would die laughing when he found out the stupendous joke that was being mounted on him.

'Peregrine, I have heard so much about you.'

His English was better than Hoomey's. He looked at Hoomey, quite understandably, as if he could not imagine why anyone would want to talk about this insignificant spotty youth, and gave him a crushing handshake. Hoomey was so frightened he could scarcely speak. He thought his hand was broken.

'Let me introduce Sir Alan Partington and Lady Partington, who only arrived yesterday. They are old friends of ours.'

'My boy!'

Hoomey goggled, as the lady who looked like a camel advanced upon him to shake hands.

'Have I met you before? I feel I have, my dear.'

Hoomey muttered something hopeless, and Angela cruised up beside him and smiled brilliantly upon the camel, and said, 'Lady Partington? How nice! Peregrine is going through a shy stage—you know how it is! When one's children are at boarding school one sees so little of them oneself—one hardly recognizes them from term to term!'

'And where does he go? What school are you at, Peregrine dear?'

'He's at Eton,' boomed Angela, when Hoomey remained stricken dumb.

'Who's your housemaster, dear? Our boys are at

Eton too, and my husband was also there, in his time. You'll have to have a little chat with him, won't you?'

'Aargh!' said Hoomey.

'I'm afraid he's not very keen on school—the ski-slopes are far more to his liking!'

'Really? Is that how he met Claudine then, and Mario?'

'That's right. Such a splendid sport for the young, don't you think?'

'It certainly is a young people's sport. I'm afraid I go up in the cable car to the restaurant, and come down the same way—I'm not afraid to admit it. But the young—well, they have such opportunities here, don't they? Are you in the English schools team, Peregrine?'

'Yes, he is,' said Angela blithely.

Hoomey's mouth opened and shut again. Did she have to overact quite so effusively? Robin was already telling Claudine's father that he was out here with a view to opening a sportswear boutique—if M'sieur Berthier knew of any suitable premises he would be interested. Hoomey had expected his two companions in deceit to sit around saying yes and no in superior voices and listening to the conversation, not setting it up and bragging about things they couldn't possibly know anything about. Now they had landed him not only in Eton but in the school skiing team—and they'd only been in the apartment about two minutes— what else was in the pipeline?

Mario was already eyeing him with a very thoughtful expression.

'May I get you ze drink, Peregrine?' he asked kindly. 'Vot you like to drink? Ze vodka?'

'No, thanks, just coke please.'

Mario poured him out a large glass of coke, topped it with several chunks of ice and, when Hoomey was looking the other way, a generous dash of vodka. The apartment was, in fact, very hot, and Hoomey drank thankfully and, quite soon, began to feel very much happier about the whole evening. In fact, very cheerful altogether.

They were invited to the table and Hoomey was instructed to sit next to Claudine, with Mario on his other side. Directly opposite was the old camel. Or the old trout, Hoomey decided.

She leaned across and said, 'I suppose you take lots of holidays? Where do you like to go best?'

Hoomey considered. 'Leeds, to my grand-da.'

Angela, leaning across her host to join in the conversation, said, 'Leeds Manor, in the Cotswolds, a delightful place.'

'The best thing about it, it's got a privy in the garden,' Hoomey said, 'with two holes in—the loo, I mean.'

'An aviary in the garden, with two owls in. A zoo, he means,' Angela trilled.

'Oh, that's very unusual. Has he got many birds?'

'No. Only my grandma.'

There was a brief, surprised silence.

Madame Berthier, rather coldly, took the lid off the soup tureen a maid had just put down before her and raised the ladle. She looked sternly at Hoomey and said, 'Consommé Julien?'

Unaware that it was the name of the soup, Hoomey said happily, 'Peregrine's the name, madame.'

He rather liked it, all of a sudden. It had more class than boring John. How did he come by it? He couldn't for the life of him remember.

The soup was dished out and Hoomey fell to, suddenly realizing how hungry he was. To his amazement the soup was stone cold. Everyone however was slurping it down, as if they hadn't noticed. He supposed it was the polite thing to do, making no comment. Eton boys were very polite. He too would force it down.

'Your cook having a night off or something?' he whispered to Claudine.

'No, ze cook 'e work very 'ard.'

'Why didn't he warm up the soup then?'

'It's supposed to be cold, stupid.' Claudine was looking at him with slight anxiety. 'You are drunk, Peregrine?' she whispered.

As Hoomey was considering this surprising statement, spoon in mid-air, Lady Partington said to him across the table, 'Your father tells me you hunt. What hunt do you ride with?'

Hoomey groped desperately for a name.

'Northend United.'

'I've not heard of that one. An Essex hunt?—is it that one with the yellow collar?'

'Blue and white stripes and red socks,' said Hoomey.

Her jaw dropped. 'I beg your pardon?'

'Granted, Mrs Trout. Or should I say camel?' Hoomey smiled warmly at her. He was quite enjoying himself after all. Why had he been so reluctant to come?

Claudine coughed loudly and drowned most of this unfortunate sentence. She whispered to him fiercely, 'Talk to Mario. Be nice to him.'

Hoomey wondered what to say. While he was cogitating a maid brought the next course which seemed to be mostly spaghetti, very long spaghetti with a bright red sauce over it. This sort of food was not in Hoomey's repertoire and he eyed it dubiously. It looked likely to be more formidable than the conversation which was now general, on the subject of the success of Claribel as a tourist resort. Count me out, thought Hoomey.

A large plate of spaghetti was placed in front of him. He waited to find out what the drill was. Mario received his. He picked up his fork, stuck it into the spaghetti and twirled vigorously. The spaghetti rolled itself round the fork in a neat package, nicely mouth-sized, and Mario ate it, more interested in the conversation than the food.

Nothing to it, thought Hoomey. He put his fork in and twirled. The red sauce flew about but the spaghetti would not take hold—it was like putting a film in the camera when it wouldn't hook on to the ratchets. Round and round went the fork but the spaghetti stayed where it was. Hoomey paused and looked round for more ideas. Everyone seemed to have the knack, the quick flick of the wrist and up smartly to the mouth, although Mario was best at it. Raised on spaghetti, no doubt. Lady Partington's dangled slightly before she sucked it all in, but the performance wasn't bad. Hoomey tried again.

The trick seemed to be to stick the fork in, lift some spaghetti and twirl with the fork tilted up, à la Mario.

This was far more successful, save the spaghetti worked its way down the fork handle and, somehow, round the fingers that held the fork. When it was all twirled in place, it held his whole hand firmly to the fork.

'Bloody hell!'

He waved his arm about, laughing.

Then he held his arm down, elbow well out, and shook it hard so that the spaghetti fell off. Some landed on his plate but quite a lot went on the cloth. He tried to pick it back off with his fork, but this was impossible, so he picked it all up in his fingers and piled it back on his plate again.

This time he decided not to tilt the fork up so far. He rolled the fork vigorously and the spaghetti took hold and started to whirl tightly into place. He lifted it up and found an enormous wad all wound up like a ball of knitting, miles too big to go in his mouth. But he gnashed at the mass and it started to slide away at great speed. He held on like a mastiff, sucking hard.

The hanging spaghetti flicked from side to side, splattering red spots in all directions, but when his mouth was full there was still a good deal hanging out. He didn't know whether to let it slip or bite it off. Biting seemed to be tidier. Strange how the stuff seemed to fly about.

He lifted his head, trying to get his breath. The conversation seemed to have come to a halt and everyone was staring at him. What had he done? He glanced sideways at Mario, and noticed that the front of his white shirt was covered with little red spots. He was just in the act of lifting his wine-glass to his lips. Floating in the wine like a live white worm was a long piece of spaghetti. Hoomey pointed with his fork, unable to speak, and started to laugh.

What a jolly funny party it was turning out to be . . . why on earth had he been so nervous of it?

But when he started to laugh the wretched stuff started to slide out of his mouth again like it had a life of its own and it was head down and suck, again, suck hard . . .

24

Jean opened her eyes and saw a star shining. It was bright and clear, unwinking, and she could not take in its meaning, her body wracked with cramp and cold. She had been afraid to sleep in case she never woke up again, yet exhaustion had overtaken her determination. Now pain needled her awake again. Perhaps she had only dozed off for a few moments. It was impossible to tell; there was no way of knowing how long they had been sheltering.

David lay heavily against her. For a moment she

panicked, thinking he was no longer alive, but then she heard the shallow sigh of his breath. She shifted, in an agony of cramp, and he gave a small groan and moved his arm.

'David!'

There had been no star before. Coming slowly to full consciousness Jean fixed on it wonderingly. It was no illusion. The snow was no longer falling and the tiny slit of sky she could see through the top of the bag was clear. She pushed her head out farther, trying to free an arm to help her. The air was icy, making her shudder. But there was a diffused light, the full moon behind the clearing clouds struggling to free itself. The mountain above was still in cloud, but the slope below them was now visible, sliding steeply down as far as she could see. True there was no piste in sight, but there wasn't a precipice either or anything too daunting.

'David!' She gave him a shove, excited by this sudden smile of fortune.

He groaned and mumbled, and groaned again.

'Hey, look, the weather's cleared!'

He took some time to come to, as she had done, but eventually took in the star and the diffused moonlight that showed them where they were.

'So?'

'We get going. We ski down,' Jean said.

'What, down there?'

'Not up, dimwit. Of course down there.'

David looked. 'For God's sake—I don't know about you, but I know my limitations, mate.'

'The sideslip,' Jean said excitedly. 'Don't you remember, if you can sideslip, you can go anywhere. That's the point of it. However steep it is, if you've got the room for your skis, you can sideslip down.'

'It was all right practising. This is the real thing. If you get it wrong—' He paused, and shivered.

'You won't. You can't. It's for real. Of course you can do it—if you don't, what else? We'll be frozen solid in another hour.'

'How do we know what's down there?'

'We don't, but down there must be nearer home than up here, mustn't it?'

'Granted. Just give me a minute or two to get used to the idea.'

They sat, pulling the bag down and moving their arms about to get some feeling back. They were numb and stiff all over.

'We'll have to do some exercises first to get the circulation going. Let's get out of this bag.'

The idea having been accepted, David started to take the initiative. They wriggled out of the bag and stood up. It was painful in the extreme.

'We must just stamp up and down until we thaw out,' David said through chattering teeth.

It wasn't easy. They seemed to have no strength at all, and moving about was agony. David, with an eye on the slope they were going to have to negotiate, presumed that, once started, the adrenalin would flow even if the blood was still sluggish. It was fearsomely steep. The more he looked at it the more impossible it seemed—to him, at least. Even while he was thinking that, he found he was reaching for his skis. It was a matter of going now, or losing one's nerve. Jean had folded up the survival bag and stuffed it away in her pocket.

'Okay?'

'No,' he said. 'But we'll go, shall we?'

'It'll be all right. Look, the sky's clearing.'

It was true, more than one star was showing now. There was a clear patch and the clouds' edges above it were outlined with gold. The ridge above them showed its ragged silhouette, glittery against the flying banners of the retreating cloud.

'You go first,' David said. 'You're best. I'll do what you do.'

'The snow's deep. The skis'll bite in. It's not like that icy piste.'

She meant easier, but David rather thought harder. But, experimenting, he found he could step down, the skis sinking several inches into the snow. Progress, although slow, was possible. Where to—that was the question? David found he was trembling with tension and anxiety—or pure funk—and tried consciously to relax. Jean was sliding neatly down below him. The slope was very steep. In his anxiety he kept turning into it, which wasn't good, and eventually caused him to take off backwards and lose control. He flung himself down in a panic, and went rolling and sliding down past Jean. Jeez, so fast! He was terrified. If he'd survived before, he'd be lucky to repeat it. If there was another drop below him he was going to be skyborne in no time.

But, by extraordinary good fortune, there was no drop below but rather a swoop up, which brought him to a halt. He lay on his back for the second time that day, amazed to be still alive. Jean was still some way above him. At least he had made good progress.

'Are you all right?' she called down.

'Yes!'

He struggled to his feet. His legs were shaking, more with weakness than fright, but he was unharmed and the adrenalin was running again. As he looked up towards Jean the moon came out from behind the ragged cloud and the snow-slopes seemed suddenly to open up all round them, satin-white and unearthly. The rocks above where they had fallen cast long shadows, inking the steepness of their descent. It was both magnificent and terrifying. What am I doing here? David wondered, his brain standing back and seeing himself, insignificant and puny, a speck in this

109

glittering moonscape. Whatever happened for the rest of his life, he did not think there was any way he was ever going to forget just this moment, taking it all in, both the beauty and the danger, and the feeling of being set apart. It was almost as if he had been blind for the whole of his life, and just got his sight for the first time. Except that it wasn't just sight, it was everything: living, breathing, feeling, knowing . . .

While he was standing in this trance gazing at the skyline Jean came down with one of his skis. He hadn't even noticed he had lost one.

'Lucky I kept my eye on it, or we might never have found it. Then we'd have been in trouble.'

'Don't you reckon we're in trouble now then?' David enquired.

She smiled, she actually smiled. 'Maybe.'

David saw that she was on a high, like him. Maybe—maybe the high would see them through, before hunger and exhaustion caught up with them.

'Downhill all the way,' she said.

'It's amazing.'

'Yes. Fantastic.'

He put his ski back on, and realized that the slope which had stopped him was the end of the very steep bit they had fallen over. The way now was easier.

'I think I can see a post,' Jean said. 'Look, down there.'

She pointed with her ski stick.

David couldn't, but knew his long sight wasn't much good. Jean set off again, side-slipping quite fast now that the slope was easier, and David knew he just had to keep up with her. It really mattered now. Perhaps, because it mattered so much, he found he was beginning to get the hang of it, sometimes slipping, sometimes stepping, sliding forwards, sliding back, but keeping his balance. Confidence was every-thing, a little success to ease the tension. Being screwed up made the legs ache and throb; to relax suddenly made everything come together.

'It's a piste,' Jean said suddenly. 'It's marking a piste!'

'Are you sure?'

Jean waited until he slithered down beside her. They were looking down now into a deep valley, and on the other side, against the snow, they could see the pylons of some sort of a lift. The slope they were on seemed to divide, steeply down to the left, which they both felt was the way back to Claribel, and more gently to the right, in the direction of the head of the valley. The post was some way down the right-hand slope.

'There's another one below it, can you see?' Jean said. 'It is marking a piste, I'm sure. Shall I go down and have a look? You wait here and I'll give you a shout.'

'But this left-hand one seems to be going in more the right direction.'

'The right-hand one must be going down as well. They both do. But I can't see any posts marking the left-hand one.'

'No. Okay. We'll go right. Lead the way.'

The slope, although covered in fresh deep snow, started off gently and Jean traversed easily down towards the post. When she got there she could see quite clearly the posts lower down, marking a long curving, gradually steepening slope down into the valley. It was just what she had hoped for—to come out on another piste. It surely led back to Claribel?— there was nowhere else it could go. The only drawback—and she thought it best not to mention the fact as David staggered alongside—the posts were painted not green for easy, or blue for intermediate, or red for advanced, but black, which meant for very experienced skiers only.

'This the main road home then?' David called out cheerfully.

Pascale had said, 'If you can sideslip, you can go anywhere.' Now was their chance to prove it.

'Yes,' she said firmly. 'Straight down to Claribel!'

She stood with her back to the post as David came snow-ploughing down, so that he didn't notice the colour of it. She was frightened, but there was no going back now. They just had to make it.

25

Hoomey let himself into his bedroom at Claridges and lay back on the bed feeling dizzy and altogether peculiar. The bedroom was empty. Jazz was downstairs with the others listening to the tale Robin and Angela were spinning, and David was lost on the mountain with Jean Woods. They said a search party was still out looking, or had gone out again, Hoomey wasn't sure which. It was serious and nobody seemed to have gone to bed. Miss Knox had gone up to the cable car station with the rescuers' back-up party and Sam was talking to the police. Big Brenda was being motherly in the kitchen to some of the more tearful and frightened girls, and Betty Dubois was dispensing cocoa and crisps to all and sundry in the kitchen.

It was midnight. The snow had stopped and the night was now clear and starry, which had prompted the rescue party to reassemble. Hoomey lay on the bed thinking about David and Jean being alone up on those frozen, glittery slopes somewhere, and a funny feeling settled in the pit of his stomach. His awful day was over and the dreadful week had nearly finished, but tomorrow he had to do the slalom competition.

Mario Cellini was going to look out for him—and how was he going to get out of that? It occurred to him, deep down in his dizzy subsconscious, that if David and Jean were still lost tomorrow the competition would probably not take place. He considered this situation as best as he could in the circumstances, and came to the conclusion that he could not possibly wish them to die merely so that he could miss the competition; he wasn't quite as self-centred as that. Were they in danger of dying? He did not know. There seemed to be quite a lot of shouting and some laughter echoing through the chalet, although certainly the atmosphere was different from usual, more twanged-up somehow. There was a definite air of nervous tension.

Hoomey had a bad headache, a bad conscience, and knew he could not possibly sleep the way things were. He got up miserably to go and join the others, although he had no wish to hear Robin and Angela's hysterical recitals of what had happened at the Berthiers—he had had enough.

He looked at himself in the mirror in passing and thought he looked rather odd. When he stopped and examined himself he saw that he had a bright red moustache, as well as a garish red lower lip and spots all over his chin and cheeks, not to mention the front of his cashmere jersey. That bloody spaghetti! He must have looked like that the whole evening and everyone too polite to mention it . . . nothing to what else had happened though. Robin was regaling his audience with it when Hoomey arrived in the kitchen.

'Some time during the evening Mario managed to corner Claudine in the kitchen alone, so old Hoomey goes in and squirts a whole bottle of soda water over him.'

'She told me to,' he protested. 'Protect her, I mean. It's what she uses me for. He was trying to kiss her.'

'What happened?' The others were agog.

'It went in his eyes and he stepped backwards, trod on the cat and sat in a bowl of trifle.'

'He was wearing the most exquisite pair of trousers, and they were quite ruined,' Angela said happily.

'Hoomey, you are fantastic!' Nutty said, her eyes shining with admiration. 'I would never have believed it of you!'

'He was drunk,' Robin said.

'I never! I only drank coke!'

'Mario kept putting vodka in it when you weren't looking. I saw him.'

Hoomey was amazed. Is that why, at the time, it all seemed such fun? Is that why he felt so awful now?

'That serves him right then. He must have been rather cross.'

'Raving,' Robin agreed.

'He's going to get his own back on me,' Hoomey remembered. He recalled the manic expression on Mario's face after the fiasco, Claudine helpless with laughter, tears running down her cheeks. Mario's threat had come through clenched teeth.

'He hasn't much time, only tomorrow. He's scoring the slalom competition,' Nutty said.

'Betty asked him back for the prize-giving tomorrow night. And Pascale and Gerard and Claudine,' Mark said, grinning. 'He'll have plenty of opportunity.'

Hoomey groaned. Tomorrow looked like being worse than today, and earlier he would have said that that was impossible.

'And when we were leaving,' Robin said, 'M'sieur Berthier shook hands very politely and said, "It's very strange, but I was expecting an Egyptian gentleman." I couldn't think what on earth he meant, but when we were coming home in the car it dawned on us—we should have remembered—Harrods was bought by an Egyptian a few years back. He knew all the time!'

Hoomey groaned again. Everybody but him thought the whole evening a real lark.

But when Robin and Angela had departed, the tale told, and they were told at last to go to bed as there seemed to be no news forthcoming about the fate of Jean and David, Hoomey felt as if the day had lasted forever. He went upstairs with Jazz and got gratefully into bed. But when Jazz put the light out the moon shone in through the window, silvering David's empty sheets. Staring at it, Hoomey could not sleep, for all his headache and exhaustion. Where was David now? The jokes were over, and total disaster seemed perilously close.

26

The beginning of the black piste was beguilingly easy; a wide swathe of snow in a shallow curve following the side of the valley very gently down. But the valley's steepest walls were at its bottom end; it seemed to narrow and close in, as if the river on its floor decanted into the main valley at the bottom by means of a waterfall or a gorge of some sort. Jean guessed the way down there was likely to be black indeed . . . Below the gorge the tree-line started, and somewhere behind the crags, Jean was convinced, lay Claribel. Not a word to David. Confidence was all, and he was descending in long laborious zigzags, crouched over his skis, keeping his balance admirably. Jean kept behind him, finding the skiing very easy. The sky was bright with stars now and all the clouds had rolled away, and she felt very alive, and frightened, and was aware that she was travelling, as it were, on borrowed strength, drawing on reserves that were fuelled by fear and determination rather than food and rest. She kept thinking of her father. She felt he was with her, his spirit skiing at her side, and the fantasy steadied her and gave her courage.

The slope gradually steepened. David's turns became more frequent and eventually he stopped because he couldn't make the turns any more. The slope was too steep.

'I'll have to sideslip,' he apologized. 'It scares me rigid, turning down that. Do you want to go ahead?'

The piste had narrowed considerably and now became a steep shelf on the hillside with the side of the mountain making a wall on the left and the other edge of the piste formed by a sheer drop down into the river below. They could hear the water cascading over rocks far below, not a reassuring sound.

'God, that scares me!'

David knew that losing control here might mean going over the edge.

Not a funny thought. The snow on the piste was fairly deep, so he contrived a method of sliding and stepping and generally fudging a way down, keeping as near as possible to the inside. He felt desperately tired and had to keep stopping as his legs ached and trembled.

Below, the piste seemed to level off and then drop dramatically out of sight. Feeling rather sick, David approached it without joy. He too had noticed that they were on a black piste but, like Jean, was saying nothing. Survival was all. Jean was ahead of him, gazing down.

'What's it like?'

She shrugged, then shook her head.

David reached her, and saw why words had failed.

The piste went down what he knew was called a gun-barrel, which meant it was a sort of slide with high sides: one was supposed to whoosh down, travelling from side to side, turning at the top of each bank like a manic skateboarder. The gun-barrel was full of snow and, unlike the bit they had just come down, there was no way of falling off the edge, but it was very, very steep, and narrow.

'I think we take off our skis and walk down,' Jean said.

David's heart fluttered with relief—the thought had never occurred to him. But when they tried it, they found that the surface was not uniformly hard, and, although for a few steps it would bear them, it would then give way and leave them floundering up to the hips. Carrying the awkward skis, and progressing in this exhausting manner, they made slow and arduous progress and what remaining strength they possessed began to ebb away. While Jean kept doggedly going, David did not want to give in, but he soon knew that he was at the end of his tether. However determined his mind, his body was failing. What he really felt like doing was to burst into tears.

'I don't think I can go much longer,' he said, trying to make it sound as conversational as possible.

'Nor me,' Jean replied.

But the gun-barrel below them seemed to open out, the terrain appeared to change once more, and the prospect of something better was too tempting to resist.

'You never know—it might be an easy swoosh right down to the village. We might have done all the black bits.'

'Do you think?' David was doubtful.

'At least, it's easier down there, not worse.'

David didn't think it could be worse.

'Unless it's just going straight down, I don't think . . .' He knew he hadn't the strength even to put a turn in any longer.

'No. I know. We'll try it—just a little way, until we

can see round the mountain a bit more, and then if it's no good—'

'We can rest up a bit.'

'Yes. Bivouac again.'

They struggled on, and as the gun-barrel flattened out the river came into view again below them, the tumbled rocks that had hidden it smoothing away, and the eager roaring of the torrent no longer distant, but close at hand. The piste widened and beckoned, smooth and shining in the moonlight.

'Look!' said David suddenly.

They could see farther down into the main valley now, and a light had come into view, winking across at them from a point on the far mountainside. It was far away, but an immediate boost to the spirits, the first sign of life, an intimation of civilization below.

They stood staring at it longingly. When they stopped they were both aware of their utter exhaustion, and the light seemed to tease and dance, so far away, but full of hope. But, only pausing to take it in, they were soon shivering with the bitter cold. David felt that, although they had come this far, it might still be in vain. He felt he had only to fall now, to slide down through the soft snow, and no power on earth would get him to his feet again. Even if all the lights of Claribel appeared spread out below, they could still fall and freeze to death before anyone found them.

'What shall we do?' In spite of himself, he could not keep the despair out of his voice.

Jean felt desperate too. What would her father have done? He had known far more about survival than she did, but he had died. He had died taking a chance. But she remembered him saying, 'Nothing ventured, nothing gained.' He had done more in his short life than many who had lived twice as long.

'Try it,' she said. 'Snowplough down. It might go all the way. I'll come behind you.'

118

The suggestion that it might, indeed, be just an easy run all the way down to lights and warmth and blessed rest, spurred David's determination to one last effort. He laid his skis out and forced his boots back into the bindings.

'The snow is soft. You won't go too fast.'

How did she know? But David poled himself into action and faced his skis straight down the middle of the piste. They started to run quite gently and he could control his speed by snowploughing without any trouble, little effort being required. The ease with which—at last—he was making good speed was gloriously uplifting . . . out with the heels, steady, steady, and sweetly round the bend, and still the deceptive slope rolled away before him into the darkness, wide and bright under the starry sky. The bitter air bit his bare face and his eyes started to water. Gently, he was going too fast. He pressed his heels out and checked himself, but had to keep pressing all the time to keep from getting out of control.

He tried, tried hard, but the strength in his legs had given out. He started to gather speed. The slope glittered and sang in the moonlight and his skis carved down through the snow in showers of bright crystal spray that he admired even as the fear started to pulse in his bloodstream. Tears blurred his eyes as his speed quickened. What could he do? He could hear the hiss of the skis under him. It was both petrifying and magnificent. Faster and faster, and the white slope seemed to spread before him across the whole face of the universe, beckoning him on, and he had no idea how to resist.

He couldn't resist. Whether he hit a bump or whether his legs just gave way . . . it was inevitable. One moment he was hurtling down the mountain on his skis, the next he was still hurtling but the skis were gone and he was rolling, sliding, crashing, gasping . . .

hurting—oh, God, hurting! He cried out. The snow went into his mouth, the snow buried him and he was still sliding, and trying to scream, and failing. Failing.

Jean watched. She was terrified. The accident happened too far away for her to see clearly, but she saw the skis fly up and the body suddenly catapult to one side, heard the thin scream of despair. Then there was silence, and the snow still and shining and beautiful and no movement on it, no sign of life anywhere.

Her last shreds of hope and optimism were obliterated.

'No!' she screamed. 'No! No! No!'

It had been her idea. She had sent him on. Her father had taken a chance and died. And now David—

She had to go down now and find him, and what could she do? She knew nothing about death, about injury. She was shaking with fatigue and helplessness. It was all finished. Only the light on the far mountain shone steadily, mocking her.

She realized she was wailing and crying out, 'Daddy! Daddy!'

He had died under the snow because he took one chance too many. But she knew now that there was no help forthcoming from any thoughts of her father: she was on her own. She stopped wailing and weeping and made a great effort to pull herself together. She had to survive, for God's sake, even if David was—

Was what? Snow was a soft landing, however violently one fell.

She shouted with all her remaining strength, 'David! David!'

Her voice echoed down the slopes and came back to her from far away on the other side of the valley, thin and reedy, fading and eerie. Surely everyone would hear her, the people whose light shone so steadily— they would come and look? She shouted again, but the mocking repeat filled her with even greater despair. It was the loneliest, saddest echo in the world. She knew she had to put on her skis and go down. She might end up out of control like David . . . she had to do something.

Her hands were numb and she was trembling uncontrollably. She laid out her skis, sideways on the slope as they had been taught. As she did so, the echo came back.

Yet she had not shouted again.

She straightened up and stood motionless, listening. It came again, a shout, faint but clear from way up the mountain behind her. She looked back the way they had come, up the face of the gun-barrel which looked quite sheer from below. The moon was shining over the top, and beyond she could still see the ridge of the mountain they had fallen over. What a long way they had come! She must be hallucinating, to think there was anyone up there.

But something moved at the top of the gun barrel, a tiny speck. The shout came again. There was no mistaking it, its echo reverberating from all the surrounding peaks.

She nearly fell over in her excitement. She screamed back up the slope, 'Here! Down here! I'm here!'

And the tiny speck moved, the voice pinged down the gun-barrel again, and the figure started to ski down. Not walk, as they had done, but ski at an astonishing rate, carving a tight track in tiny flicking turns from side to side. Jean watched, trembling with excitement and relief. Tears flooded down her cheeks, and yet she was laughing at the same time.

'David, David!' she kept saying. 'They're coming, they're coming!'

Her legs were so weak she sat down in the snow and hugged her knees, still laughing and crying. The skier fairly hurtled towards her, twisting constantly so that he made a track like a corkscrew, his arms held high with sticks flashing in the snow-spray. Just like the brochure, thought Jean crazily—but it was night-time, and in the brochure the sun shone all the time. This was for real. The skier stopped right beside her in a great shoosh of flying snow. She saw the teeth gleaming in a happy smile.

'So, we find you!'

It was Gerard.

Jean was helpless with relief and joy. Gerard! Her nightmare had turned into a fairytale. Gerard had a rucksack on his back and a walkie-talkie which he was already speaking into, not even breathless.

'David has fallen—tell them—David—' Jean pointed down the slope. 'I think he's hurt. He didn't get up.'

Gerard put down the walkie-talkie. 'How long ago?'

'Only a few minutes. Just before you shouted—I was shouting to him, and you answered.'

'Yes, I heard you—that's how I found you.'

He talked some more into the radio, carrying on a two-way conversation at some length. Then he closed it down and turned to her.

'I make you comfortable, then look for your friend. You will stay here until the sledge comes.'

He worked very quickly, shrugging out of the rucksack he was carrying and unpacking a thermos of hot soup, and a duvet sleeping bag. He helped her to a secure place against some trees below the piste and wrapped her up and poured her some soup.

'I hurry, you understand—your friend—perhaps he need me more. My friends come for you, do not worry. Now—'

He pulled the duvet up over her head and tucked it firmly round her and gave her chocolate and glucose tablets.

'Do not move! They come for you.' Then, with a smile, 'You are very lucky. Or perhaps very clevair! I do not know. Afterwards, you tell me, eh?'

Jean nodded blissfully. Gerard clicked back into his skis, shrugged the rucksack back on, and was gone, straight down the slope like an arrow from a bow. Jean watched him go, hugging her knees.

'David, be alive!' she whispered. 'Be alive, like me! Be alive!'

27

When Hoomey woke up it was light, the sun was shining, and he was alone. Jazz's rumpled bed was empty and David's was too. It hadn't been slept in. Hoomey turned over and tried to remember what was going on. His first thought was that his dreadful dinner party, for better or for worse, was behind him. This lightened his heart considerably. Then he remembered that he hadn't yet thought of a way to get out of the slalom competition, which immediately stopped his heart getting lighter and made it plummet again. Then he remembered the significance of David's empty bed, and he was back to square one, deeply depressed and wishing he was back home with his mother, who would be bringing him a cup of tea in bed.

The chalet was very quiet, as if everyone were sleeping off the late night. Nobody had gone to bed much before midnight, and no news had come of Jean and David. Hoomey lay there wondering if they were dead. He could not imagine any of his friends dead. He wasn't clever enough. This was supposed to be a fun holiday.

But while he was still considering this Jazz came back, whistling.

'It's all okay,' he said. 'They're found, rescued. They're heroes. David's a bit wonky, bashed up—he's in the clinic but should be let out this morning. Jean's there too, but there's nothing wrong with her. She wants to do the slalom. She's a nutter.'

Hoomey found this news very cheering, in spite of his other unresolved problems. Thinking they were dead had been a far more serious depression than his other depressions. His other depressions now seemed relatively minor. However, such being the nature of life, now that they were the only ones to think about, they grew quite quickly, even while he was getting dressed.

'How can I get out of this slalom competition?'

Jazz was lying on his bed, eating one of Hoomey's Mars bars.

'You can't, Hoomey old man, you can't.'

'I could go to Claudine's.'

'What, and meet her ma, after last night?'

'Mmm.' Good point. The memory of the spaghetti reared its ugly head. 'No, perhaps not.'

'Miss Knox will send out another search-party if we're not all present and correct. Our teachers had a bad night last night. They need to have an easy time today. We must be nice to them.'

'Mmm.' Fair enough. Suppose they had had to go home with two missing? Even Hoomey could see that this was not a nice thought.

'It's only for beginners. We'll push you off, then you can fall over gracefully and slide to the bottom. Mission accomplished. Nothing to it.'

'Do you think?'

Certainly, the way Jazz put it, it sounded a doddle.

'Yes, I do think. And first we're all going to have a farewell lunch in the restaurant at the top station—no, not the very top'—seeing Hoomey's new pang of apprehension—'the first one. Easy run down from

124

there. Through the slalom poles. You don't want to miss that, do you?'

'No.'

'Well then. That's the programme. Stop worrying and enjoy yourself.'

Hoomey could not believe that life could suddenly become so simple again, but on reflection it seemed that Jazz was right—only one slightly awkward moment to face at the top of the slalom and then that was it—next stop, home. The week was nearly gone and all his anxieties with it. Pity he hadn't done much skiing . . . perhaps they would have another trip next year. He found he was quite looking forward to it.

While they were still scoffing breakfast, David and Jean were delivered back to the chalet. While everyone cheered and banged their spoons on the tables, the two 'survivors' looked incredibly embarrassed, and were glad to sit down and be given baked beans and hot tea. Apart from David being covered with bruises and having a black eye, they seemed to be none the worse for their adventure.

Betty Dubois announced a 'grand party' that same evening.

'We will have some celebrities to supper—Mario Cellini and Gerard Marchand will give the prizes for the slalom competition, Pascale and Claudine are invited, and we have decided to make a presentation to the Rescue Services after all the support we received last night, so some of their members will be present too—altogether a very special occasion!'

'What do we want to have Mario for?' Hoomey complained.

He had been hoping never to set eyes on the man again. After the soda water siphon incident, Mario had said a great deal, although as it had been in Italian Hoomey did not exactly understand it. He had, however, definitely got the general drift. This hadn't taken a lot of intelligence.

'He wants to get his own back on me.'

'You pinched his girl-friend, no wonder.'

'I didn't! I didn't—'

'No, but it looks like it, doesn't it? Claudine chose you, Hoomey, you've got to admit—not me or Mark or Preston or anybody, but you. Great privileges like that don't come without strings, do they? Stands to sense. You've made an enemy.'

Well, only till tomorrow, Hoomey thought.

It seemed that Mario was not very popular anyway, not only with him—Hoomey. When he had got a message after the Berthier dinner party that a rescue party was out on the mountain he had refused to join it, although he was supposed to be one of its committed members. Pascale said, 'Well, no one would be around to admire 'im, would they? 'E would not be interested.'

The weather was now sunny and kind again, and the skiing classes set out with a fun day to look forward to. Hoomey bravely joined Pascale's group once more to spend what was left of the morning—everyone had got up rather late after the excitements of the night before—practising slalom on the nursery slopes. For this the poles were set in a line down the slope and one had to zigzag in and out of them to the bottom, the fastest being the winner. Pascale warned them that the competition in the afternoon would be down a somewhat steeper slope and that everyone should be able to do this baby one without any trouble.

'Even Hoomey.'

However Hoomey managed to get a ski on either side of the first pole and got hung up on a very tender part of his anatomy, and when Pascale came to the rescue and removed the pole he shot off out of control across the slope straight for a group of very smart

French ladies with a group of toddlers on skis. They fended him off with unladylike screams of 'Merde!' and he disappeared on his back over a far hillside. Jazz was dispatched to look for him.

Hoomey was at the bottom, making for home, his skis over his shoulder.

'Don't put yourself out for me,' he said hopefully.

'It's a pleasure, Hoomey,' Jazz said politely. 'If we go up on the cable car we'll meet them at the top just in time for lunch.'

The view from the restaurant was of sparkling slopes and much activity, as the hordes of instructors whizzed about on skis carrying poles and markers and flags, laying out the courses for slalom, for downhill and jumping. There was even an area for 'hot-dogging' where Pete was going to attempt to turn a somersault on skis in his first competition. Hot-dogging was acrobatics on skis and everyone was keen to watch it, after they had competed first in their passing-out slalom.

'Hoomey'd do well in that. Why don't you enter?' Mark enquired provocatively. 'Your skis are always in the air.'

Nutty whispered, 'Don't you worry, Hoomey. I'll look after you.'

Hoomey really stumped her at times, so deep in his rut that he was scarcely visible. Where had he been when the normal genes for ambition, rebellion, optimism and aggression had been handed out? Down in his bunker, presumably.

The beginners' slalom had a long queue for it; it wasn't just for their own class. The course was on a very wide and quite steep piste. Beyond the slalom was the downhill course, down which ace skiers were whizzing exactly like Ski Sunday, with large crowds watching who clanged cowbells and yelped like rabid dogs. The downhill disappeared over a fearsome brow out of sight. Somewhere below there was the ski-jump, also with a crowd of spectators. Only the beginners' slalom, to Hoomey's great relief, was not of much interest to casual viewers, being attended merely by the instructors and hangers-on, a very bored Mario with a stopwatch on the finishing line, and Gerard helping at the start. (Probably because Pascale was on duty there.)

'All you've got to do is fall over quite quickly and slide to the bottom,' Jazz said to Hoomey, as they put their skis on outside the restaurant. 'Piece of cake. Lot'll do that, no one will know if you do it on purpose.'

Hoomey thought he'd probably do that before he ever got to the start, as waiting in the queue on a steep hillside on a pair of skis was extremely difficult. Jazz stood on his downhill side and Nutty on his uphill side, like prison warders. When Hoomey dropped a glove and bent down to retrieve it, he started slipping backwards down the hill, but the two of them grabbed him before he was out of reach and hauled him back up again.

'I don't know how you do it, Hoomey!' Nutty said. 'I don't know how—' She was going to say 'anyone could be so stupid', but thought better of it in time.

Their class shuffled gradually to the head of the queue. Everyone went down mostly according to form: Jean Woods perfectly, and fast, David steadily, slowly but safely, Preston with great panache, taking two poles with him, Mark elegantly, with showing-off turns, spraying up the snow, to show how beneath him the beginners' slalom was. At the bottom he went to make a snazzy, snow-spraying halt, crossed his skis and fell over. Nutty nearly took off laughing.

'You next, Hoomey.'

Gerard and Pascale came forward to help, the difficulty being to get the skis facing down the slope and be in balance ready to start. Between the four of them they bodily manhandled Hoomey into his starting position. Pascale looked worried, as well she might, Hoomey about to show off to all and sundry that he had spent the week eating creamcakes in Claudine's flat. Miss Knox stood smiling fondly.

'Look as if you're enjoying yourself, dear!' she called out in a jolly voice.

'Enjoy yourself, dear,' Nutty hissed in his ear, as they all let go.

Gerard put his hands over his eyes. Pascale groaned. Jazz and Nutty stood rooted, aware—of the four of them—just what Hoomey could get up to in the disaster stakes when he really put his mind to it.

So well had they done their job, so well balanced was he as he sped off down the slope that he decided not to fall over at all, but—as Miss Knox instructed—enjoy himself. If he missed a few poles, so what? He flew past the first one at such speed that he quickly realized—miss a few poles . . . he was definitely going to miss the lot, for no way was he going to be able to turn at such impressive speed. It was just like the time he had homed in on Sam—a magnificent feeling but, deep down, an uneasy fear about coming to a halt.

'Oh, mon Dieu!' moaned Pascale.

'Jeez!'

Jazz gazed in awe as Hoomey sped towards the crowds lining the Downhill. His sudden shouts of dismay caused the spectators to look behind—at which they opened up like the waters of Babylon parting, and Hoomey zoomed through on to the icy piste of the Mens' Downhill.

Spectators lower down thought he was the fastest yet and a great clamour of cowbells and yodelling went up as he hurtled down. He disappeared over the brow of the hill and the cheers echoed up the slopes—a newcomer of such talent! Who was he?

His friends at the top gazed into the far distance, hanging on every shred of sound to try and monitor his progress. They heard the cheers suddenly stop, and a great sigh went up. They all gazed at each other in despair. There was a long, long silence.

''E 'as fallen!' muttered Pascale.

Indeed he had, deep into a pile of snow at the side of the piste. A soft fall, better than he could possibly have hoped for, he clambered out with a sense of great relief—only to find that he was facing an enormous crowd of people, all staring at him. He was deeply embarrassed, to think that he now had to ski away nonchalantly in front of all these eyes. He straightened up, skidded, and started to slide away in his usual hopeless manner out of control, backwards.

He could not understand why he found it so much easier to ski backwards when everyone else went forwards. But there was very little he could do about it and as he gathered speed once more down the piste he found he was faced by lines of people three or four deep on either side all gazing at him in great astonishment. And as he went, faster and faster, they started to cheer again and bang their cowbells and make their astonishing yodelling noise, egging on this competitor who could go faster backwards than all the others could go forwards.

Why did this happen to him? Hoomey couldn't fathom it. Naturally he quite soon disappeared backwards into the snowbanks that edged the next bend on the course, and when he had fought his way out of that he found himself sitting on the outside edge of the piste where it curved away to hurtle downhill at an even more frightening angle. For a moment he was safe, and he did not move, savouring the peace.

However, some stewards were shouting at him and waving him to get out of the way. When he looked back the way he had come he saw the next competitor hurtling down the piste towards him, obviously intending to take the curve on the outside edge very close to where he was sitting.

The sight unnerved him utterly.

In his panic he got up, which he knew immediately was a mistake. His skis took off again, apparently having a life completely of their own. Being nailed on board he had no option but to go too. The skier missed him by inches, leaving a sulphurous tirade of bad language behind him—even in a foreign tongue there was no doubting its meaning—and Hoomey found himself following in his tracks, once more to cowbells and flag-waving. He could not believe it—not again!

Ahead of him the piste forked. One way, the way the skier ahead had taken, went headlong down but the other way curved in a far more encouraging fashion not over the brow but along its top, disappearing into the trees. It was quiet up there, and Hoomey willed his skis to go that way, his desire so great that it was as if they actually heeded him, keeling away off the desperate downhill and running smoothly across into the blessed peace of a wide, tree-lined, easy piste. Hoomey couldn't believe his luck. The greenest of green runs, it slipped him away from all those awful yodellers and flag-wavers into a smooth and easy coast down. Like silk, his skis ran—he was relaxed, bending his knees, even laughing because it was all such a relief.

'I'll tell them when I get down,' he was thinking, giggling happily.

'Beginners' slalom! I did the Men's Downhill!' He wouldn't add, backwards.

The slope he was on seemed to give out on to another, wider piste. It was hard to see exactly what happened, but there seemed to be more of the flag-waving crowds ahead.

'Catch me doing that again!' he thought, and eased

into what was supposed to be the famous snow-plough.

Funny, but so relaxed had he been skimming between the peaceful trees that he had not realized that the run was more downhill than he thought, and his unpractised snow-plough seemed to have very little effect on his speed. He tried more earnestly, crouching down, bottom well out, but only succeeded in going faster. The piste curved round, travelling ever more steeply and joined another run, where the crowds were clustered again. Hoomey saw a skier flash down in front of him, crossing his path. Ahead of him was—not a comfortable thick snowbank to provide a soft landing—but a large crowd of spectators craning to see where the skier had gone.

As he came round the bend Hoomey saw instantly where the skier had gone, and where he was now about to go.

The piste plummeted down, reared up slightly, and stopped in mid-air. The skier ahead of him was just in the act of taking off for a jump, leaning into the sky with his arms down at his sides, just as seen on television. The crowd whooped.

Hoomey screamed.

The crowd whooped even louder.

Hoomey's skis started to run, and in the whooping of the crowd his screams of terror were quite unheard.

28

Nutty made a bosh of her slalom, knocking two poles down, but Jazz came down behind her looking as if he had made a very good time. Gerard and Pascale followed them down, their party having finished. They stopped in an anxious group.

'We must find Hoomey, see if he's still in one piece,' Nutty said anxiously.

'He might have won the Men's Downhill,' Jazz said.

Gerard left them to go and compete and Pascale led the way down to go and look for Hoomey. Jazz and Nutty followed, both aware that this was nearly their last run, savouring it to the full, and vowing to do it again, whatever the cost. Pascale, after having lost Jean and David the day before, was in a great state of nerves about Hoomey.

'Zey will take away my certificate! I lose my job! I lose all my pupeels!'

'No, no,' they soothed her. 'It's not your fault—not Hoomey. He's — he's sort of — of —'

There wasn't really a word for Hoomey. Not many came like him.

When they got to the bottom they took off their skis and went to look for Hoomey. They tried the Ambulance station first but he wasn't there, nor had they heard of him, which allayed their worst fears. They then tried the chocolate shop—no Hoomey.

'He'll be back in the chalet,' Nutty suggested.

But they none of them wanted to go back to the chalet and miss all the fun so they decided to go and watch the ski-jumping and the hot-dogging. The bottom slopes were crowded with people. In the bright, cold sunshine it seemed as if the whole town was gathered there, packing in all the excitement before the convoy of holiday coaches and cars departed for home.

'It's always like this, the end of the week,' Potter said. 'Chaos—then they all go and there's a lull before the next lot arrive.'

'How did Pete do in the hot-dogging?'

'We'll go and have a look at the results—find out.'

The results of the day's events were posted on large boards outside the bottom station, and they pushed their way through to try and read them. All the times and results of their slalom were there, showing that Jean Woods had won their class. Jazz had done well and Nutty decided there was nothing to be ashamed of in her eleventh.

'There's Hoomey's name,' Jazz said suddenly.

'What do you mean?'

'John Rossiter. Look. First in—' Jazz screwed up his eyes, thinking he was going either mad or blind. 'Ski-Jumping—it says Ski-Jumping.'

They all stood blinking.

It was quite true. In large plain letters under the heading, 'Ski-Jumping Beginners' it said, 'First, John Rossiter.'

'There must be someone else called John Rossiter,' Nutty said. 'It's not all that outlandish a name.'

'It's not all that common either,' Jazz said.

Pascale said thoughtfully, ''E go that way, when we see 'im last.'

Potter whistled.

'You don't mean—!'

Pascale said, 'Wiz zat boy, anyt'eeng—' She shrugged and rolled her eyes.

Jazz said, 'He's never learnt how to stop, that's for sure.'

134

'Fantastic!' Nutty said. 'Bloody fantastic! If it is him—'

'We find 'im,' Pascale decided. 'We go 'ome. Back to ze chalet.'

They were all stunned, trying to come to terms with the fact that Hoomey was a genius.

They found him on his bed, quietly crying.

'I want to go home,' he wept.

'You've won the ski-jumping! Did you—did you ski-jump?' Nutty leapt on him and gave him a great shake. 'Is it really you, Hoomey?—it's up on the result board, large as life—first, John Rossiter!'

He blinked at her.

Pascale sat herself firmly down in front of him. 'Did—you—go—down—the—ski—jump?'

'By mistake, of course,' Jazz put in kindly. 'She means did you go down by mistake?'

Hoomey nodded. 'I couldn't stop!'

'There! It's true!' Nutty whistled.

'It ees impozzible!' said Pascale (with a good deal of truth).

'Brilliant!' Jazz was ecstatic. 'You've shown 'em, Hoomey—Mark and Nick and all, and old Mario— wiped them up, you have.'

'And crying!' said Nutty, in deepest disgust. 'Get up, Hoomey! You're a hero! Your name's up there for the whole of Claribel to see, large as life—first, John Rossiter. It's no time for crying.'

'I didn't mean—'

'To be a hero?'

'No.'

'You can't help it, mate! It just comes naturally. You're a flaming marvel, Hoomey, honest. You can go home covered in glory. Just think what your mother'll say!'

Hoomey thought, and began to look rather more cheerful.

'You won't tell her—'

'You couldn't stop? As if we would!'

'I didn't want to—'

'You never do, Hoomey, that's your trouble,' Nutty said.

'Let's go back and find the others,' Jazz said. 'Tell 'em you've won the ski-jumping! Fantastic!'

They all congregated in the chocolate shop, where Claudine was waiting for them, along with Mark and Nick and Jean and David and most of the others. Hoomey had to tell his tale, and the others all fell about, and then decided, like Jazz and Nutty, that he was a hero, and Claudine kissed him, and at this point Mario Cellini arrived with Gerard, and came over to the table where they were all sitting.

'You 'ave seen ze results, Mario?' Claudine asked sweetly, with her arm round Hoomey.

Mario looked at Hoomey with his black-fire eyes narrowed to ominous slits and said nothing.

'You are coming to ze prize-giving, Mario? Madame Dubois she expect you. She want everybody. You come?'

He replied in sharp French, and then turned to leave them. Bending down to Hoomey's ear he then said, softly and with great venom, 'I make sure I see you tonight!'

Hoomey blinked.

Nutty, sitting opposite and missing nothing, said 'Cor! Whatever did he mean by that?'

Hoomey's new-found complacency was shattered. No one else but Nutty seemed to have noticed the exchange, which had sounded to Hoomey very much like a threat.

Nutty, seeing his alarm, pretended quickly that it meant nothing.

'To say goodbye, I expect. He wants to see the back of you, Hoomey—too much competition!' She laughed her strident laugh.

Hoomey was already deciding to give the prize-giving a miss. He could say he felt tired and go to bed. Another eighteen hours and all these dreadful dangers would be over—he could not wait for the moment when they all piled back into the bus again. Nobody else seemed to have his troubles—they were all too busy looking forward to the prize-giving which was going to be the grand finale after supper.

When they got back to the chalet Madame Dubois was in a panic, wanting to get the supper early and re-arrange the dining-room for the festivities; everyone was ordered to get their packing done in good time and extra hands were needed for making dainty sandwiches to hand around amongst the guests. General chaos prevailed, amongst which Hoomey, seeing David flaked out on his bed, catching up on the lost sleep of the night before, decided to follow his example and opt out. At least he was safe in his bedroom.

Jean, following Miss Knox's orders, was also lying on her bed, supposed to be getting some rest in before the evening's fun. It was true she was exhausted, but she was so high on both love and achievement that it was impossible to lose out on such bliss by going to sleep. She wanted to spin out this glory for ever, and go over and over in her mind the memory of coming down the mountain the night before with Gerard.

When the sledge had come down with two more of the rescue party, it was decided that David should be taken down on it with its two handlers, and that Gerard would escort Jean. After the rest, the hot soup and chocolate and buoyed up by the bliss of being in Gerard's care, Jean had assured them she still had enough strength left to ski down. Gerard led the way and she had kept close, and the astonishing experiences of this eventful night culminated in this last, blissful ski down the mountain with Gerard.

She lay on her bed gazing up at the ceiling and reliving every moment of that magic descent. With all the danger past, and the knowledge that she had come out of a bad situation with honour and credit, the landscape of satin-white snow glimmering under the full moon changed from one of stark hostility to unearthly beauty. The ice-cold air stung her eyes as she focused on the graceful back before her and she was not sure if she was crying for joy or relief, or whether the tears were part of the crystal landscape glittering and freezing on her cheeks. She then wished the way down was never-ending and the necklaces of lights that came into sight round the next bend of the lonely piste—the town that they had so longed to see earlier—were not as welcome as they would have been earlier. But Gerard kept turning round to smile and encourage, and her skis hissed over the snow: she never let him down, skiing right down safely to the bottom station, where a whole crowd of people was waiting for them. After that her memories were slightly confused. Gerard faded away and it was a doctor and a nurse, and Miss Knox, and the police, and great, overwhelming floods of fatigue that blotted out all the pains and glories of the day.

It was nearly over.

She had won the slalom, and Gerard was going to give her a prize later. She would see him again, and perhaps he would talk to her for the last time, and then it would all be over.

But nothing would ever be the same again. Jean did not know whether she was happier than she had ever been in her life before, or whether the exhilaration that filled her mind was merely the symptom of a gigantic discontent—tomorrow she was going home!—back to a life which now seemed more like a grey sleep than a meaningful existence. Somehow she had to make sense of it all, and not let opportunities slip; she had to come back to the mountains again, or there would be no point in living.

29

After supper all the tables were pushed back and one was placed strategically on the far side of the dining-room where crowds were forbidden.

'All the audience will sit here, the good side, next to the inside wall,' Betty Dubois hissed at the Spotty Boys, 'so the weight will be right. Then only the prize-giver will be at the bad end, and one person going up to receive their prize. It should bear two people all right. Make sure the dignitaries sit at the side, not too near the table. The Mayor is coming and the Rescue, remember. If you put the chairs out for them . . . It will only last about twenty minutes, so make sure when it's over everyone stays this end . . .'

The shaky house was a perpetual worry, but Betty reckoned the week had been a great success. Even the drama of the night before—with its happy ending— had served to get her place mentioned in the papers and on the news. Every little helped. The Mayor and the Rescue were coming to show the flag—a public relations gesture, and it was all luck that it was centred on the Chalet Clair Ciel.

The school party was in very boisterous spirits, this being their last night, but their teachers got them settled in their places, Claudine and Pascale arrived, and then the dignitaries, and last of all Mario and Gerard, who had been competing in the Downhill. Gerard had won it and Mario had come second.

Seeing Mario's scowling face, Hoomey wished bitterly that Gerard had let him win. It surely would have improved his frame of mind. As it was, his eyes went immediately to Claudine and her inseparable companion, Hoomey. Hoomey had tried to sit inconspicuously in the kitchen, but had been hauled out by his so-called friends, because Claudine was asking for him. If only he hadn't won a prize, he could have stayed decently out of the way . . .

The room was very hot and still smelled of chips frying. The condensation dripped down the windows and the icicles made pelmets outside, glittering in the intense cold of the night. The excited whispering stopped as Gerard and Mario took up position behind the table. They had a load of certificates, and a large cardboard box. 'That's the gold cup for the Ski Jump, Hoomey!' Nutty leaned across Claudine to whisper loudly to him. 'That's yours, mate, bet you!'

First of all Miss Knox stood up in her place and gave a long spiel of thanks and congratulations to all the right people . . . how happy they had been, etc, etc. Then the Mayor stood up and said how 'appy they had been to 'ave them, and then the head of the Rescue stood up and said 'ow 'appy they 'ad been to rescue them, and Betty Dubois said their visit had been a pleasure and may there be many more, and Sam said loudly, 'Hear, hear!' and stamped his bad leg by mistake, ending with a sharp groan.

'Now, the prizes.' Miss Knox fumbled with her list, and everyone cheered.

Gerard nobly gestured to Mario to present them, and Mario stepped forward with his smart smile. He was dressed in a silver and black track suit with a gold chain round his neck and a very flash silver watch, more bracelet than time-piece, and was obviously aware of the doting admiration coming his way from the Sylvie Parker contingent. He smirked in their direction. (Rumour had it that he had pinched Sylvie's bottom in the queue for the cable car, but most considered that that was only Sylvie swanking. 'More likely Preston,' Nutty commented.)

Everyone got a certificate of competence, even Hoomey. When he went up to receive it everyone cheered and stamped their feet.

Mario bent over to the blushing Hoomey and said softly, 'I 'ave something for you after.' He gestured to the large cardboard box. 'A present to remember.' He leered in what Hoomey thought a thoroughly evil manner. 'At the end.' He shook Hoomey's hand with an agonizing pressure, and Hoomey stumbled back to his seat. He thought of pretending to be ill, but the chairs were so squashed together it was very difficult to get out again in the middle of the speechifying, especially with Claudine squeezing his crushed hand and being proud of his having won the Ski-Jump.

The Head of Rescue was now making a speech about the amazing courage and presence of mind of Jean Woods and David Moore when they had fallen off the mountain the night before and managed to get down safely almost to within sight of Claribel before the Rescue found them. Apparently it was very impressive: 'Many peoples 'ave died in the same circumstance,' said the Rescue. 'Peoples wiz far more experience.'

Everyone clapped and cheered again, and the red-faced couple had to go up to receive a special present from Gerard.

They each received a matching set of woolly hat and ski-gloves of undeniable quality. David had a warm handshake from Gerard, but Jean received an embrace and a kiss.

She thought she would die of the glory. The hot room whirled round her head and the noise of cheering and the boys' whistles seemed to come from far away as she remembered the magic ski down with Gerard.

'You must come back,' Gerard was saying, 'I talk to you afterwards. Your teacher tell me who you are. I

141

skied wiz your father, I did not know you was the daughter of Macey Woods. I see now where you get the courage and the determination! I am proud to know you, cherie.'

What more could she wish for? It was as if God had opened up Heaven to her and given her the run of his blessings. She stumbled back to her seat in a complete daze, seeing and hearing nothing. David was grinning and still blushing, but proud too, even as he realized that his parents wouldn't understand in a thousand years what this week had meant to him, even if he were to spell it out for ever.

The noise of the cheering died down and everyone sat forward expectantly as Mario picked up the cardboard box. Gerard moved away and came to sit at the back, his duty done, leaving Mario alone at the table. Mario was smiling in a very self-satisfied and ominous way.

A hush fell.

Hoomey felt very sick and started to tremble.

'We now 'ave one prize left,' said Mario.

He picked up the cardboard box and lifted it high in the air.

'A very suitable present for my friend Peregrine. Please, Peregrine . . . come 'ere to receive your present!'

'Peregrine! Peregrine!' everyone yelled, loving it.

Hoomey got up and was pushed and shoved along the row of chairs and out to the front. He walked like a zombie across the large open space of the room to the lonely table and stood, visibly shaking. He could not speak.

Mario put the box down on the table and fumbled inside. A lot of tissue paper flailed out and Mario pulled out a large object and held it high.

It was a white chamber pot, with roses on the side.

'To ze bottom skier!' said Mario.

There was a sort of stifled silence. Hoomey gawped;

someone tittered; and then, without any sort of warning or preamble, Mario, still holding the chamber-pot aloft, started to slide backwards away from the table. Hoomey felt a strange surge under his feet and thought he was probably going to faint with embarrassment, but instead he felt himself literally sinking through the floor. Mario was going too, with a sort of amazed look on his face, as if things weren't turning out the way he had planned. Still holding the chamber-pot aloft, he vanished.

Betty Dubois screamed, her worst fears realized.

Quite slowly and majestically the whole side of her chalet dining-room fell off and slid down the hill into the river. With it went Mario and his chamber-pot, the table, and Hoomey. The floor then cracked apart and the part on which all the rest of the guests were sitting was left where it belonged, but now open on to the cold and starry night, the rushing of the torrent below and the bright lights of the town on the other side of the river.

Apart from the moans of Betty Dubois, there was a long, amazed silence. Everyone stared at the town lights, not quite appreciating what had happened. Then Miss Knox said quietly, 'Lucky we invited the Rescue,' and the Rescue recovered from their shock and started shouting at each other with much Gallic excitement, waving their arms to indicate that everyone should retreat to safety in the better half of the chalet.

'Move quickly and quietly!'

Miss Knox took up battle stations, standing on a chair and conducting the retreat, while Big Brenda helped Sam, no doubt thinking that, with his luck, if anyone were destined to follow Mario and Hoomey into the river it was he.

'Lor', what about poor old Hoomey?' Nutty said anxiously, having been prevented from peering over the edge of the wreckage. 'Let's go out the front and whizz down to the river—he might be drowning!'

Naturally it was too much to expect such interested parties not to want to see what was going on and most of the school got their anoraks and rushed outside to spectate. The wreckage had all slid down the steep slope into the river, the brick piers holding the outside wall up having collapsed: windows, window-frames, the timber wall, guttering, part of the roof and bits of the floor had all gone adrift, and lay scattered over the banks and in the water. Of Mario and Hoomey there was no sign.

The Rescue men lost no time in rushing down the bank to search in the water. Nutty, Jazz and David followed them.

'Cripes, he could be killed!'

The snow was deep and the water icy and fast. Some of the wreckage was trapped between rocks, causing the water to foam furiously at the blockage. There was no sign of bodies or life, and the chief of the Rescue held up his hand abruptly for silence.

'Écoutez!'

Somewhere from amongst the debris, faintly over the roaring of the water, could be heard thin shrieks for help.

'C'est Peregrine!' shouted the Rescue.

'Hoomey! Hoomey, where are you?'

The Rescue shooed Hoomey's friends back and they could only stand and watch as the men started to scrabble away in the direction of the shouts. Hoomey seemed to be in the river, underneath a part of the wall with a window frame hanging on to it. The men levered up the timber and one man went in underneath and started to send out an excited commentary and they all homed in and started throwing out great lumps of timber in all directions. Apparently Mario was in there as well.

'He's probably holding Hoomey's head under. No wonder he's shouting,' Jazz said.

But no—great excitement!—Hoomey was apparently holding Mario's head up out of the water. Mario was unconscious. The two of them were dragged out and a stretcher was brought for Mario, and Hoomey was delivered back to the chalet, dripping wet, shivering and groaning. Showers of excited French followed him.

''E is the 'ero!' Pascale translated for the benefit of the unbelieving Nutty and Jazz. 'They find him wiz ze Mario in 'is arms—'e keep 'is 'ead out of the watair!'

'Formidable!' shouted the head of Rescue. He was clapping Hoomey on the back and clasping his hand.

They gave Hoomey a large glass of brandy, and made him have a hot bath. Mario was dispatched to the clinic, and the Rescue proceeded to nail up the doors in the chalet that gave into the demolished dining-room.

'What shall I do without a dining-room?' moaned Betty Dubois.

'We'll have to have breakfast in bed,' Jazz suggested hopefully.

The chalet rocked to the sound of hammering and cheering and general abandonment. Hoomey, wrapped in enormous bath-towels, sat next to the kitchen fire, woozy on brandy, and said to Nutty, 'I wasn't holding his head up out of the water. His silver bracelet had got caught up in the back of my jersey and I was trying to get disentangled.'

'Ssshh!' hissed Nutty. 'Don't tell anyone, you twit! Let them think you saved his life.'

'I would rather—'

'SHUT UP!' said Nutty firmly.

Claudine came in and put her arms round Hoomey and gave him a hug.

'Peregrine, tu es merveilleux! Je t'adore!'

145

'Yes,' said Hoomey.

"E tell me—you 'is 'ero!'

'No,' said Hoomey.

'Yes,' said Nutty firmly.

'You win ze Ski-Jump and you save ze life of Mario Cellini! Mon petit Peregrine!' She gave him another hug, rather akin to Mario's handshake. Hoomey looked at the clock on the kitchen wall and estimated only another sixteen hours before the bliss of getting back in the coach and starting for home.

'I want to go to bed,' he whispered to Nutty.

30

The next morning Big Brenda brought in the local paper over breakfast (they were all squashed together in the kitchen) and showed it triumphantly to the room. Their French was just about good enough to see that 'Peregrine Plunket-Masham-Blandford-Fitzpatrick saves the life of Mario Cellini' was in large print on the front page, together with a flashlight picture of the wreckage in the river, a portrait of the chief Rescue and one of Mario skiing as on a brochure advertisement.

Hoomey turned scarlet and said, 'I—'

'You did, Hoomey! It says so!' shrieked Nutty.

'You're a hero, Rossiter!' beamed Sam.

Even Mark Parker was looking stunned and impressed, and everyone was looking at him as if they were glad to know him. Hoomey wanted to die.

'Here, you must take this copy home for your parents,' Big Brenda said to him. 'I can buy some more.' She pushed the paper into his lap. 'Your parents will be so proud!'

How to explain his name, Hoomey wondered? They would never believe it was he—he would do nothing to convince them either. Only a large hole in the back of his best sweater where the wretched bracelet had got hung up was proof of his side of the story, and his mother would be very concerned about that, having bought the sweater new for the holiday. He would wear it neatly darned for the rest of its natural life and would be forever reminded of the prize he so truly deserved—but never quite received—that of Bottom Skier. He sighed deeply.

Nutty gave him a derisive glare. 'Hoomey!'

Jazz grinned. 'Leave him alone, Deirdre darling. You can't change nature.' He gave Hoomey an affectionate nudge. 'This time tomorrow, mate, we'll be almost home.'

Hoomey smiled gratefully and his eyes lit up. Jazz laughed.

They all went skiing for the last time (except Hoomey who decided he was suffering from delayed shock) and after their last lunch on the mountain, skied down and took their gear back to the ski shop. David and Jean went together, and walked back to the chalet in silence, taut with regret. Yet wonderful memories overcame sadness; it was a strange mix of tangled desires and agonies. Best of all, for Jean, Gerard was back at the chalet with Pascale, drinking coffee in the kitchen.

He got up when he saw Jean. 'I wait for you! I want to say—'

He took her elbow and guided her out of the mob, into what passed as a lounge, at that moment filled with luggage waiting to go on the coach.

'Last night, the accident—I had no chance to say . . . but I told you I only discover yesterday you are the daughter of Macey Woods. He was my friend! I ski with him in winter, I climb with him in summer, many times. Also, I help look for his body, after the avalanche, I bring him down the mountain. He was older than me, but he was great friend. Now, I have a letter here you give to your mother, and if she want to come visit me, and you too, there is my address. My parents receive you with great pleasure, both of you, even if I am away. You come any time, you understand?'

Jean took the letter, unable to think of anything sensible to say. Gerard said, 'Now, I go—I 'ave a class waits for me!' and he kissed her on both cheeks. 'Bon voyage—au revoir!' And disappeared.

'Oh, David!' Jean said weakly.

'Cor!' said David.

Jean had to sit down on the nearest luggage. She didn't know whether to laugh or cry. Her legs were trembling, but whether with love, excitement or surprise she did not know.

'I reckon I'll have to become a brother to you,' David said. 'Muscle in on the family invitation! That's some offer!'

Even to David, without the invitation, everything that had once seemed unattainable now seemed to fit into the realms of the perfectly possible. Although leaving it now was tough, he knew without a shadow of a doubt that he was coming back, whatever it cost him in effort, bantams, mucking-out or whatever. And Jean had her ticket: no wonder she looked as if she had taken leave of her senses.

'We haven't packed yet,' he reminded her gently.

'Oh, David!' was all she could say, dreamily, as he marched her upstairs.

They all milled into the coach at teatime, and Claudine, Pascale, the Spotty Boys and Betty Dubois lined up to wave them goodbye. Betty was beaming, having discovered that she could get her dining-room repaired on the insurance; her day was made.

Big Brenda helped Sam into the coach, and Miss Knox stood by the steps fiercely counting them in, crisply efficient as ever. She missed Hoomey because he had already been sitting in his seat for an hour, clutching the last of his Mars bars and gazing happily into space.

'He's here, miss!' they all shouted in reply to her enquiry.

'We're all complete then.' She turned with relief to Mr Singh, who closed the doors and started to back out neatly from beside Sir Alan Partington's Rolls Royce. They all waved and cheered madly.

The coach started to slip away.

Hoomey dug his teeth into the last of his iron rations and turned to Jazz at his side.

'Great, wasn't it?' he said.

ALLY, ALLY, ASTER
Ann Halam

Richard and Laura aren't very keen on making friends with the next door neighbour's pale, cold daughter, Ally, when they move to the isolated cottages on Cauldhouse Moor. There's something strange, almost inhuman, about her. But it's only as the bitter winter winds and snow draw in around the bleak moors that Richard and Laura discover that Ally is more than a little icy . . .

FINN MAC COOL AND THE SMALL MEN OF DEEDS
Pat O'Shea

Finn Mac Cool is the bravest, wisest, tallest and rudest of the warriors of the Fianna. Unfortunately, when the giant arrives to ask for his help Finn just happens to have a very bad head-ache. He is the only hope for saving the heir to the throne in the country of the giants so Gariv, the sly old servant, has to use all his wiles to get Finn on his feet and ready for battle.

RACE AGAINST TIME
Rosemary Hayes

From the moment Livvy sees the island, she knows there is something wrong. A strange and menacing force beckons, drawing her and her brother into a race against time. They are destined to fulfil an ancient quest to restore a magical cross to its rightful owner, but they must face the forces of unparalleled evil to do so.

SNAPS KELLY AND THE PAPER MONSTERS
Joseph Ducke

Snaps Kelly lives with his decidedly eccentric grandpa in an equally eccentric house in London. Snaps is a fairly ordinary boy, until one hot summer the paper monsters arrive! Suddenly he has to become an ace detective, determined to discover why all the paper in London is dissolving. With no newspapers, no underground tickets, no toilet paper(!) and worse still, no money, daily life is changing dramatically. Meanwhile, the evil Dr Chengappa is always one step ahead and it looks as though life in the civilized world could be changed forever.

A PACK OF LIARS
Anne Fine

When Laura's teacher sets up a pen pal scheme, Laura finds herself in correspondence with an extremely boring girl called Miranda. Desperate, Laura decides to liven things up by pretending to be a Lady Melody from a noble and wealthy family. Her friend, Oliver, is horrified at her pack of lies and makes her feel so guilty that she tries to make amends by visiting her pen pal personally, only to discover that Miranda is a professional thief who steals from the rich to give to the poor! The plan to expose her makes entertaining and gripping reading.

ROSCOE'S LEAP
Gillian Cross

To Hannah, living in a weird and fantastical old house means endlessly having to fix things like heating systems and furnaces, but for Stephen it is a place where something once happened to him, something dark and terrifying which he doesn't want to remember but cannot quite forget. Then a stranger intrudes upon the family and asks questions about the past that force Hannah to turn her attention from mechanical things to human feelings, and drive Stephen to meet the terror that is locked away inside him, waiting . . .

MIRACLE AT CLEMENT'S POND
Patricia Pendergraft

When Lyon and his friends find a baby abandoned by Clement's Pond it seems common sense to leave it on the doorstep of the poor old village spinster, Adeline, who has longed for a baby all her life. All the children think it's the perfect answer to the problem at the time, but as Lyon is to find out, there are unforeseen complications to follow.

LAURIE LOVED ME BEST
Robin Klein

Julia hates the hippie-like commune where her mother has taken them both to live. And Andre feels stifled by her father's rigid ways. Together they seek refuge in an abandoned cottage behind their school and begin to make it their ideal home. However, their private lives amazingly remain a mystery to each other, so when a gorgeous 18-year-old boy turns up, they're soon unwittingly competing for his charms.

LIONEL THE LONE WOLF
Linda Allen

While travelling by train to visit his Uncle Richard, Lionel overhears two men plotting a murder – or so he thinks. The worst part of it is, his uncle is their target! Being a fast-thinking private investigator isn't as easy as Lionel had imagined. But then he suddenly has a brilliant idea and, with the help of his uncle, 'the lone wolf' cracks the mystery.